ELEMENTS OF RETROFIT

THE THOMAS ELKIN SERIES : BOOK ONE

N.R. WALKER

COPYRIGHT

BLURB

Book one in the Thomas Elkin series

Generation versus generation, traditional versus contemporary, these men are about to learn a lesson in architecture and love. Can they prove that the old and new can be the perfect design?

A successful New York architect, Thomas Elkin, almost has it all. Coming out as gay and ending his marriage before his fortieth birthday, he needed to start living his life. Now, four years later, with his relationship with his son back on track and after a few short-lived romances, this esteemed traditional draftsman thinks he knows everything about architecture, about life.

Cooper Jones, twenty-two years old, is about to take the architect world by storm. Talented, professional, driven, and completely infuriating, Cooper is the definition of a Millennial.

Starting an internship working with Thomas, Cooper is about to knock Tom's world off its axis. Tom can teach Cooper about the architecture industry, but Cooper is about to teach Tom what it means to live.

DEDICATION

To my husband.

For not always understanding my need to do what I do but putting up with it anyway.

ELEMENTS OF RETROFIT

N.R. WALKER

CHAPTER ONE

Definition: Retrofit—To substitute new or modernized parts or systems for older equipment: fit in or on an existing structure, such as an older house; substitute new or modernized parts or equipment for older ones.

LOOKING out of my office window over the darkening New York City skyline, I could see my reflection in the wall of glass before me. Beyond the expensive suit and shoes, there was gray hair at my temples—my once-black hair was now salt and pepper—and there were creases at the corners of my eyes.

Forty-four years old. *Forty-four. How did that happen?*

It seemed like I'd missed half of my life. In many ways I had.

The light on the intercom flashed. "Mr. Elkin?"

My receptionist was fifteen years older than me and had been working with me for ten years, since the day I'd started at the firm, and yet she never faltered in her professional etiquette.

"Yes, Jennifer?"

"Ryan is on line two. Would you prefer I take a message?"

"No, it's fine. I'll take it." I pressed the speaker button. "Ryan?"

"Hey, Dad, yeah, it's me."

"Anything wrong?" I asked. It was unusual for him to call the office. "Still coming for dinner?"

"Yeah, yeah, it's all good. Just about dinner," he hedged, "I was wondering if you'd mind if I brought someone?"

This surprised me. Since his mother and I had separated, it had taken a while for things to get back to normal between us.

"Yes, of course, that's fine," I replied. "Someone special?"

"Oh no, nothing like that," he said with a laugh.

I could hear muffled voices in the background.

Then he added, "Just ran into an old buddy from school. He just got into town. He's by himself, and I told him he could have dinner with us."

"Okay, that's fine," I answered. Ryan was very social, and growing up, he had forever had a crew of friends who'd lived at our place as much as their own. I'd quite often arrived home late to a den of high-school kids pretending to be asleep. I looked at my watch. "See you soon.

I disconnected the call and pressed Jennifer's line. "Can you please order dinner for three to be delivered to my place?"

"Certainly. Thai? Italian? Japanese?"

"You choose."

"Very well."

There was a soft click in my ear, and I went back to staring at the evening skyline for another half an hour, before packing up my laptop and walking out of the door. Jennifer gave me a polite smile. "Japanese delivered to your door at seven-thirty."

I smiled warmly at her. "Thank you, Jennifer."

"Have a good weekend, Mr. Elkin," she said, knowing I'd be working both days. I worked most weekends. "I've taken the liberty to have lunch delivered for you tomorrow. Security will bring it up."

"Don't know what I'd do without you."

She smiled proudly. "Have a good evening, Mr. Elkin. Give Ryan my best."

"I will."

I took the elevator from the top floor of executive offices down to the executive marble lobby, walked a block to the executive marble lobby of my apartment building, took the elevator to the executive suite on the top floor.

Expensive. Polished. Predictable.

Those three words just about summed me up.

I'd been preoccupied lately, unsettled and lacking *something*. I'd quite often caught myself staring out of the window for some lengths of time, not able to recall a single thought. Maybe I needed a vacation. Maybe I'd take one after this next big contract was done.

I loved my job as an architect. Loved it. I loved the lines in structure, the quiet confidence in well-built, historical buildings, and I loved the superiority and functionality of modern design.

I loved my apartment, had some good friends, and I even had an amicable relationship with my ex-wife, all things considered. My relationship with my son was better. Good, even. We'd had a rough patch when his mother and I had first separated five years ago, but now at twenty-two years of age, he could see all sides of the situation and had made peace with it. With me.

No sooner had I put my briefcase down, changed into jeans and a button-down shirt, and poured my first glass of wine, there was a knock at the door. I checked my watch, and knowing the doorman would have sent Ryan straight up, I called out, "It's unlocked."

"Hey, Dad," Ryan yelled from the door.

I could hear a quiet conversation and I remembered he was bringing company. My apartment was a large, open floor bachelor pad, and the kitchen ran along the inside wall, out of the line of sight from the front door.

"In the kitchen," I replied. "You boys want a drink?"

Ryan walked in, followed by a face I didn't recognize at first. "Dad, do you remember Cooper Jones?" Ryan asked by way of introduction. "We went to high school together."

The name yes, but he didn't look a thing like I remembered. Gone was the gangly, awkward teenager, replaced by a fit-looking young man. He had messy, short brown hair, a wide smile, and mischief in his hazel eyes.

"Yes, I remember," I said, extending my hand for him to shake. "You just grew up."

Ryan rolled his eyes. "That's what happens, Dad, when you don't see someone for five years."

Cooper shook my hand firmly. "Nice to see you again, sir."

"Can I get you boys a drink?" I asked again. "Dinner will be here in about half an hour."

I had my wine, they opted for a beer, and Ryan told me how Cooper's family had moved to Chicago and how he'd lost touch with him through college, but Cooper had come to New York City for the summer. He'd literally checked into his room and gone in search for something to eat when he'd run into Ryan, who had then pulled out his phone and called me to see if he could tag along for dinner.

"Hope you don't mind," Cooper said with a smile. "I was only going to grab something passable as food from a 7-Eleven or something."

My nose scrunched up at the thought, and Cooper laughed, telling me, "That's the same reaction Ryan had."

Dinner arrived, and as we ate, the two boys talked about people they knew. Although the conversation almost excluded me, I didn't mind. It was good to see Ryan laugh, and their college stories were rather funny. Very different from me when I was twenty-two, that was certain.

Ryan looked at me. "You're quiet tonight, Dad." He pulled at the label on his beer. "How're things?"

I think he wanted to know how things were with Peter but didn't want to ask outright in front of company. "Good," I said, not about to say I was single again after I'd told Peter I wasn't interested. "Work's been busy."

He got the message because he gave a nod and went back to picking at his beer label.

Changing the subject, I looked to Cooper. "So, what brings you back to New York?"

"I have a summer internship," he said. He was just about to speak again but was interrupted by Ryan's ringing phone.

"Hey," Ryan said loudly into his cell. "Hell yes, I'll be there. I'm bringing an old friend of mine who just got into town... Okay, see ya soon." Ryan clicked off the call and looked at Cooper. "Man, you *have* to come out with me tonight. We got tickets to the hottest new club."

Cooper shrugged and grinned. "Um, sure."

Ryan looked at me somewhat apologetically. "Sorry, we'll need to cut it short tonight. Hope you don't mind."

"No, I don't mind at all," I replied. And I didn't. Hell, at twenty-two I'd been married with a baby on the way and a house in the 'burbs. It wasn't until I'd almost hit forty that I'd realized what I'd missed out on, what I'd spent twenty-five years hiding...

"Go out. Have a great time," I told them. "Be careful. And if you need a place to crash in the city, there's always here."

"Thanks," Ryan said with a genuine, appreciative smile. But then his brow creased. "You sure you don't mind?"

"Mind?" I scoffed. "I'm jealous!"

He laughed, though I doubted he knew the underlying truth to my words. I *was* jealous. I was jealous he had a social life. I was jealous he still had his youth, without the weight of mistakes and life wearing him down.

They left to spend their Friday night out doing God knew what while I tidied up after dinner, sat down with a glass of wine, and opened my laptop, spending my Friday night working.

I WAS in the office on Monday early, like always, and had forgotten about the intake of interns, until Jennifer buzzed me on the intercom. I looked up from the job specifications. "Yes, Jennifer."

"Sorry to interrupt, Mr. Elkin," she said. "If I could trouble you at my desk for a moment."

The only time Jennifer ever asked me to come to her

desk was when she wanted me to have a visual of a client—or opposition—before I met them. "Sure," I told her.

Jennifer's desk ran along the left-hand side of my double doors, which ensured no one got to see me without checking in with her first. I opened the door and she handed me a file, which I took. "Interns," she said quietly. "There are three to choose from. That's them over there." She looked pointedly toward the waiting room without moving her head.

I looked over to see two young men and one woman, all eager to impress and impeccably dressed. Usually the four executive senior partners got to choose from the top four candidates, so I knew any of the three remaining candidates were good. I read through the very brief credentials lists first, not even looking at names or gender. I just wanted talent.

Academically, they were all relatively evenly matched, but then a name stood out. I risked a glance at the suited man who I hadn't even recognized as the kid who'd had dinner in my apartment just three nights ago.

He looked different. Gone was the backpacker look. Gone was the kid who drank beer and talked about drunken antics with my son.

In his place was a professional, serious man, dressed in a well-tailored suit.

Without another thought, without *any* thought, I looked at Jennifer, handed her the file, and said two words that would change my life.

"Cooper Jones."

CHAPTER TWO

JENNIFER KNOCKED ON MY DOOR, and upon walking in, introduced the man behind her.

"Mr. Jones, this is Mr. Elkin. He's a senior partner here at Brackett and Golding. You will do everything he asks when he asks you to do it. You'll be here when he gets here. You'll be here until he leaves. Keeping up?"

"Yes, ma'am," Cooper answered.

Jennifer sniffed. "You may call me Jennifer," she told him, then looked pointedly at me, signaling to the young man that he should address me.

In that split second, I wondered if he'd acknowledge that he knew me or knew Ryan, at least, and I wondered if I'd done the wrong thing by taking him on.

But he gave a curt nod and said, "Mr. Elkin, it's an honor."

I smiled at his professionalism while Jennifer turned on her heel. "Right, come with me. I'll show you to your desk."

Cooper didn't smile, but his eyes flickered with humor before he followed her out of the door.

And for the next two weeks, I worked with him every

day. He mostly worked with my team, but sometimes with me—sometimes for minutes, sometimes for hours. He was efficient, dedicated and very talented. For his age, he was one of the best I'd seen.

For his age. I had to keep reminding myself he was only twenty-two.

But even with the mundane jobs he was doing as an intern, it was easy to see he had a love for architecture, much like I had when I'd been his age. Much like I still did.

He would use his hands animatedly to describe something, and his eyes would light up as he spoke. He was passionate, that was for certain.

And as an intern, I should have had him doing what the other interns were doing—the mundane tasks, still ensuring they learned, but interns basically did the little jobs no one else wanted to do.

The other senior partners rarely saw their interns, and granted, before Cooper, I'd rarely seen any of mine. But he was different. He had an energy, a presence. I didn't know what it was, but I was intrigued by him. He was fascinated by the work that went on around him, and that was refreshing.

Maybe because he was an old friend of Ryan's, or maybe it was because of his love for architecture, but instead of having him learn from other people on my team, I picked him to work closer with me.

It was his second week there, late in the afternoon, and we'd had a staff meeting in the conference room, which turned into a bit of a concept meeting, then became a design think-tank. I liked those meetings. More casual, open, and everyone was encouraged to discuss problems, allowing group discussions on possible solutions.

Cooper was merely an observer. He never said anything

unless spoken to. His answers were well thought-out and calculated. It showed a professional maturity that surprised me, considering his age.

The other staff came in and out, all busy with their own schedules, and by the end of the day, I found myself sitting alone with him at the large oval table.

"So, how are you finding your time here?" I asked just as the last person was walking out.

"Oh, I love it," he said quickly. "Everyone's great, very helpful. I tend to ask a lot of questions..."

I smiled at him. "An inquisitive mind."

"When I'm learning something, yes," he said. "And there's an awful lot to learn. I think I've annoyed a few of your draftspeople."

He made me laugh. "Good. Pick their brains. Ask them anything."

"I have already." He shook his head, as though he couldn't believe something. "It's surreal, you know, that some of the most recognized buildings in New York have their blueprints framed on these walls. That I'm walking past them like they're just pictures... but they're not. They're real."

I was still smiling at him. "Some of them are incredible."

"Oh, they are," he said. He was so excited. "The Woolworth building is amazing. The original blueprints are on the wall," he said, shaking his head again. "I can't believe it."

"Well, that's a little before my time," I told him.

"Have you designed any?" he asked. "That are framed on the walls?"

"Sure. Come on, I'll show you." I stood up, and by the time I got to the door, he was right beside me. "All of the blueprints framed on walls were at some point either designed from original concept or had some work done on them by Brackett and Golding," I explained as we walked down the hall. "The company's one of the longest continuously trading architectural firms in New York. We've put our stamp on quite a few."

"Very traditional, very prestigious," Cooper said. "In design and in reputation."

I stopped walking and stood in front of one particular set of framed blueprints. Cooper stopped with me but looked at me as though he might have said the wrong thing. I pointed to the gilded frame.

His eyes popped. "The Radiator Building?"

The fact he knew the name of the building as soon as he saw it made me smile. "It's now called the American Standard Building, but yes, the Radiator."

"You worked on it?" he asked in a whisper. His eyes were still wide as he stared straight at me.

"Not when it was originally built in the twenties. I'm not *that* old," I said, and he smiled. "But I worked on it in the late nineties, when it became the hotel it is today."

Cooper's mouth fell open. "It's stunning." He looked from me to the blueprints, as though he was mesmerized. He lifted his hand to trace his fingers over the drawn lines. "The black brickwork is brilliant. How it minimizes the contrast between walls and windows, and in the 1920s, it was such forward-thinking. And the gold on the tower..." His words trailed off. He shook his head again and pulled back his hand. "Sorry. I get carried away."

I stared at him. The way he spoke of architecture, of buildings, of the art in them was something I did. It was a passion in me, something that no one else really understood.

"Don't ever apologize." My voice was barely a whisper.

Cooper's eyes stayed on mine, intense and vivid,

making my heart thump erratically. It wasn't until someone walked past us that our connection was broken.

Something had just passed between us. A familiarity. An understanding. A moment.

I exhaled loudly and took a step back from him. I needed to put some distance between us. "Here, look at this one," I said, pointing to another frame down the hall. "It's more modern."

"The Citigroup Center?" he asked with an amazed laugh. "You worked on it too?"

"Not me personally," I told him. "Hard to believe, but even the seventies were before my time. But it's one of my favorites."

Cooper laughed out loud. "I didn't mean anything about your age," he said, still smiling. "I just can't believe all these buildings came from designs out of this office."

"It's incredible, isn't it?" I asked. Then I nodded to the blueprints in front of us. "See the angled roof line? They wanted to setback penthouses in the angled roof, but couldn't due to zoning restrictions. Now it houses a computer-controlled tuned mass damper, a four-hundred-ton block of concrete that slides on a thin layer of oil. The inertia of the damper reduces the swaying of the building by up to forty percent."

I stopped talking when I realized now it was me who was babbling on about the wonders of architecture. "Sorry, I get carried away," I said, repeating his words back to him.

Cooper smiled at me, but his eyes bore straight into mine. "Don't apologize," he said quietly. He stared at me. His gaze never faltered, and I was unable to look away. After a long moment, he broke the connection by turning back to the blueprints. "That is some incredible engineering."

I cleared my throat. "Yes, it is."

Then I looked around to find nearly almost everyone else in the office had gone. I checked my watch. "I didn't realize it was so late."

"Is there anything you need me to do?" he asked.

"No." I had work to take home but didn't mention it to him. "I think we might call it a day."

Cooper looked around, as though checking we were alone. "Can I ask you something?"

I had a feeling this was not a work-related question. "Yes," I answered, hiding the caution in my tone.

"Did you take me on because of Ryan?"

I blinked at his blatant question. "No," I half-lied. "I took you on as an intern because of your credentials. You were top of your class."

He nodded and smiled. "I didn't want to be here on some favor, that's all. I mean, it's a dream to work here. I'd just hoped that I earned my place."

Cooper was honest, almost to a fault. He spoke transparently. If he thought it, he said it. I liked that trait in people. I liked it in him.

"I'm sure you have," I told him. "I've been watching you. You have a very good eye for detail."

His face brightened and he tried not to smile. "Really?"

If he was asking if he really had an eye for detail or if I'd really been watching him, I wasn't sure. I couldn't believe I'd just admitted to it. Instead of answering him, I gave him a smile and turned to walk back to my office. "Have a good weekend, Cooper."

"Same to you, Mr. Elkin," he called out behind me.

I packed up my briefcase and walked out of the office with Jennifer. "Any plans for the weekend?" she asked.

"No, just the usual." Which meant work. My usual was work.

"If you need anything," she said, "you have my number."

I smiled. Dear Jennifer was the sweetest woman. She organized my entire professional life and sometimes my personal life too. She knew what food I liked from which restaurants, she knew what cologne I wore, she knew birthdays, anniversaries, and did it all without looking up from her computer.

"I'm sure I'll be fine," I told her. "But thank you. You're really worth more money."

She smiled, and just before we went our separate ways on the sidewalk, she said, "Don't work too hard."

Every weekend, and most nights, was about work for me. I'd had a slew of one-night stands. I'd tried dating. And in the beginning, after the separation from my wife, it had been exciting. It had been new and exhilarating and everything I'd dreamed it would be.

I tried *everything*, once, sometimes twice. I did it all—safely, of course—but four years on and I was looking for something else. I just didn't know what. I'd met a guy, Peter, and theoretically, he should have been perfect for me. Similar age, similar interests, similar everything. But he was too passive, too agreeable to everything. I had ended things with him a few weeks before and had happily dove headfirst into work.

I had every intention of spending a quiet weekend at home, finalizing two case files. I went to the gym once, treated myself to some online porn, and ordered in food. It was perfect.

Except on Sunday night, I dreamed of Cooper.

It was vivid and hot. I dreamed I was fucking him. His

head was thrown back and his mouth was open and I was inside him. He groaned with every thrust.

It was so real, I woke up hard and aching. I could almost taste his cologne on my tongue.

I got to work a few hours later on Monday morning and almost tripped over my own feet when I saw him.

It was absurd. Ridiculous. Wrong, even. He was the same age as my son!

And yet there he stood, wearing gray suit pants and a matching vest over a crisp white shirt. His vest pulled in at the waist and showed the shape of his ass. He was talking to someone else, but he smiled at me and my heart thumped in my chest.

Fuck.

"Good morning, Mr. Elkin," Jennifer said with a bright, wide smile.

I cleared my throat and still croaked when I spoke. "Morning."

"Busy schedule," she said matter-of-factly. "First meeting at nine."

"Good." I needed the distraction. I needed work and meetings and appointments, difficult clients, and over-budget builders. Anything to distract me from a certain twenty-two-year-old man, whose eyes I could feel on me, burning into my skin, from across the room.

CHAPTER THREE

————————————

I MANAGED to avoid Cooper all day. Mondays were always busy, and I told myself I was imagining the attraction. The thought of me being attracted to him was preposterous. He was twenty-two, and I was forty-four. He was just a kid!

But every day I saw him, and every day I looked for him. In an effort to put some distance between us, I had his schedule jam-packed, and he seemed to thrive.

I'd managed to quash any notion that I could have been interested in him. The fact he spoke about my work with a passion like mine was nothing more than a professional admiration. Even in my line of work, it wasn't every day I met someone who loved architecture like I did, and it had just thrown me, that was all.

At least that was what I told myself.

It was late on the Friday evening of Cooper's third week when he dropped some files on my desk for me and looked at the board in the corner of the room. It was the first time he'd been in my office without anyone else with him. He eyed the drafting board in my office like it was the space shuttle to a young, wannabe astronaut.

The drafting board itself was rarely used these days. Nearly all drafting was done in CAD programs, which took precision to an art form, but sometimes I still liked to use the old-school drafting board and blueprints in paper.

"I've seen you eye it a few times. You can go look at it," I told him, looking up from my paperwork.

He grinned, walked over to it, and ran his finger along the wooden frame. "It's like touching an artist's easel," he said quietly.

I smiled at that analogy. "I guess it is."

Cooper looked at me, then back to the drafting board and the blueprints on it. "This is the Mosconi job," he murmured.

I stood up and walked over to him. He'd seen enough job sheets and specifications to recognize it. "Yes, it is."

"It's a beautiful building," he said, almost shyly. He traced his fingers across the elevations of the plan, along the façade of the building. "The lines are definitive. It's stream-lined and geometric. It speaks of elegance that comes with history, yet it's sustainable and retrofitted for modern living." He spoke as though he was thinking out loud. Then his eyes darted to mine and he blushed. "Sorry, I get carried away."

I'd never seen him shy or even remotely unsure of his own words. It was an emotional reaction, and I liked it. Something else I shouldn't have noticed.

I also shouldn't have noticed the blush across his cheeks or the way his chest rose and fell with each breath. I shouldn't have noticed how his eyes darkened, and I certainly shouldn't have noticed the lines of his neck, or his jaw, or those of his lips.

I had to swallow so I could speak. "Don't apologize. Architecture is a beautiful thing."

Cooper's eyes darted to mine and he held my gaze. "Yes, it is."

The air between us was suddenly static and it made my heart thump out of time. Cooper opened his mouth to say something, something I was pretty sure I didn't want to hear, so I walked quickly back to my desk, putting some much-needed space between us. *Jesus Christ.* I couldn't think, I could hardly breathe. He was just a kid, for fuck's sake. He was the same age as my son.

I shouldn't be checking him out. I shouldn't find him attractive. Or smart. Or clever. Or funny.

I shouldn't like the way his eyes sparkled when he learned something new. I shouldn't like the way his lips curled when he smiled. I shouldn't wonder what they felt like, how soft they'd feel against mine.

Oh, fuck.

I shook my head and cleared my throat. "I uh, I think..." I tried again. "I'll be working from home this weekend."

"Oh," Cooper said. I didn't know what his facial expression was. I didn't dare look at him. He sounded like he didn't care. "Okay."

"I have a few things to catch up on here, but you can finish early if you like," I said, dismissing him. I didn't watch him leave, but when the door clicked softly, I looked up to my office, and seeing it empty, I finally breathed.

I needed some space, some breathing room, to get my head cleared of this nonsense. And, like the weekend before, two days working from home where I could lose myself in my work without any distractions was just what I needed.

Only that was not what happened.

Saturday morning I got up, threw on some jeans and a T-shirt, and set about making coffee. Which became looking for coffee, which became ransacking the kitchen, pulling the pantry apart looking for fucking coffee.

Then the intercom buzzed. I cursed at the interruption and pressed the button. "What?"

"Sorry to bother you, Mr. Elkin," Lionel, the doorman, said. "I have a Cooper Jones here. Says he's working with you today."

I stared at the intercom. "Pardon?"

I heard a muffled voice, then Lionel spoke again, "Cooper Jones, sir. He says he brought the Lewington files..."

Shit. Shit. Shit. I cleared my throat. "Um..."

Lionel's voice came through the intercom. "He said to say he brought the Lewington files *and* coffee." Lionel didn't exactly sound impressed. "Apparently the coffee is important."

I smiled. "Let him up."

I opened the door and went back to the kitchen, tidying up the mess, and wrote *coffee* on the shopping list.

There was a brief knock at the door. "Hello? Mr. Elkin?" Cooper called out.

"Yes, come in, Cooper," I replied.

He walked in, carrying a messenger bag over his shoulder, and a tray of take-out coffee in his other hand. He was wearing suit pants but no tie or jacket, and his shirtsleeves were rolled to his elbows. He was looking every part the relaxed professional, while I stood there in jeans and bare feet.

He slid the tray of coffee onto the kitchen counter, and I looked at him questioningly.

"I stopped by the office and picked the files up," he said,

putting the briefcase down and sliding the bag from his shoulder. "And coffee from the café you like." Cooper looked around my apartment, from the open living and dining room to the gourmet kitchen. The furniture was expensive, probably pretentiously so, but it was a direct representation of me. It was classic and traditional, with Chesterfield leather sofas and an antique dining table. The only modern furnishing was the kitchen. Cooper took it all in as though it impressed him. Finally, his eyes landed on me. "So, where are we doing this?"

I ran my hand through my hair. "I, um... well, when I said I was working from home," I said quietly, "I didn't expect you to work as well."

"Oh," he said, realizing he'd just turned up at my apartment without an invitation. "Oh, shit." He looked mortified. "But Jennifer said specifically I was to work when you worked. No exceptions. It was one of the first things she ever said. She was rather specific."

I smiled at him. "It's fine, Cooper."

"Jennifer scares me," he admitted, still not sure where to look. "I mean, I'm sure she's nice and all, but she has a ferocious glare. She makes me nervous. Anna, one of the other interns, is scared shitless of her."

He was clearly embarrassed and rambling. I smiled and handed him one of the coffees he'd bought. "Cooper, it's fine. We'll set up at the dining table. Pull all your files out, and we'll have a look."

"I'm really sorry," he said again. "I feel like an idiot."

I laughed at him and sipped my coffee. "It's fine, Cooper. It shows great work acumen that you'd be at work at"—I checked my watch—"eight o'clock on a Saturday morning."

His eyes widened. "Am I too early?"

I couldn't help but smile at him. "No, you brought coffee, so it's all good."

I picked up my briefcase and set it down on the dining table, pulled out my laptop, and we settled into a comfortable working silence. He'd ask a question every now and then, while he worked on getting the energy compliance ratings for the Lewington job, and I spent the next few hours trying to ignore the fact that the man I'd dreamed about, whom I'd fantasized about while I'd jerked off in the shower last night, was sitting across from me.

I also ignored how he slipped the end of his pen between his lips and how he'd lean his head on his hand with his fingers in his hair. Making myself focus on my work, I somehow managed to get the specification sheet half done for the same job Cooper was working on. It was helpful to have us both on the same plans, running through the same file sheets, and I didn't realize the time until Cooper stood up and stretched. "Hungry?" he asked, checking his watch. "It's lunchtime."

I looked at my watch to see it was almost one. "Jeez, I didn't realize the time."

Cooper walked into the kitchen. "Can I make myself a sandwich?" he asked. "Want one?"

"Um, sure," I answered, not sure what I had in the kitchen in the way of sandwich ingredients.

I watched him as he rifled through the fridge and the pantry like he owned them, obviously looking for something in particular. "Have you got peanut butter?" he asked. "I can't find it."

"Peanut butter?" I asked disbelievingly. "No, I don't think so."

Cooper shook his head. "How can you not have peanut butter?"

"Um, not since Ryan was little," I said, then immediately regretted my choice of words. I didn't want him to think of me as a dad to one of his friends. I didn't want him to think I was implying he was a kid. I didn't want him to think of me as someone twice his age, or his boss, or... I didn't know what the fuck I wanted him to think.

Needing the distraction, I grabbed my keys. "Come on, we'll go out and grab some lunch," I told him. "I need to grab some coffee anyway."

"Uh, Mr. Elkin?" Cooper's voice stopped me as I neared the door. I turned to face him, and he looked down to my feet. "Shoes?"

Fuck.

"Does Alzheimer's kick in at your age?" he asked with a laugh.

My mouth fell open. "I'm not *that* old, thank you very much!"

He laughed again, then tried to hold it in. "I'm sorry, was that out of line?"

"What for?" I asked. "Making fun of Ryan's father or your boss?"

"Neither," he said. His eyes shone and he grinned. "For making fun of the elderly."

I rolled my eyes and pulled on my shoes. "So, the attitude? Is that a hunger thing?"

"Yep," he replied cheerfully. "That's an 'I'm on my lunch break and can say what I want' thing."

I walked to the door and held it open for him. "Oh, is that the same as 'you work for me, you'll watch your mouth or you'll spend the rest of your internship sorting mail' kind of thing?"

He laughed as he walked to the elevator. "You win." He

pressed the button, and after the doors opened, he stepped inside. "So, the lack of humor? Is that a hunger thing?"

"No," I said with a smile, stepping in beside him. "It's an old-age thing."

Cooper laughed. "Such a vicious circle."

CHAPTER FOUR

I SHOOK my head but couldn't hide my smile. I liked his banter. He had a certain arrogance and boldness that came with age. Or lack of it.

When the elevator doors opened, Cooper stepped out into the foyer and gave a smug smile and cute little wave to Lionel, the doorman.

I rolled my eyes. "Cut it out. He didn't let you up to my apartment because he was doing his job."

Ignoring the jibe, Cooper smiled as we walked from the foyer out onto the sidewalk. "So, what are you buying me for lunch?"

"An attitude adjustment," I replied quickly.

Cooper laughed. "I heard the little Vietnamese place up here is one of the best."

"It's one of my favorites."

"Where else do you go out?"

"I don't, really."

"Not at all?"

"I work a lot. The people I've dated don't understand the long hours."

We walked in silence for a bit, while Cooper obviously thought about what those long hours meant in the career he'd chosen.

"Does that scare you off?" I asked with a smile.

"What?" he asked quickly, looking at me. Then he shook his head. "No, no. Not at all. I don't mind the long hours."

We walked into the little café. I ordered some steamed vegetable rolls and a noodle salad to go, and I bought some ground coffee from the café Cooper had bought coffee from this morning.

The walk back to my apartment was quieter; his banter was gone. I grabbed some plates and dished up lunch for us both. The dining table had our work all over it, so we ate at the kitchen counter.

I was about to ask him where the impressive Millennial mockery had gone when he said, "Ryan told me."

"Told you what?"

He stabbed his noodle salad with a fork. "About your divorce from Mrs. Elkin."

I put my fork down and frowned. "And what else exactly did Ryan tell you?"

He took a mouthful, seemingly oblivious to my discomfort. "That it was hard on him. That it was hard on all of you."

"It was," I said quietly, still unsure of his point.

"He said you've dated a few... *people*, but nothing serious."

I cleared my throat. "Really. Is that what he said?"

Cooper nodded, took a drink from his water bottle, and pushed his empty plate away. "You know, it's not easy for anyone," he said. "Jesus, I remember when I came out to my parents, I thought they'd flip their shit."

I blinked. Twice.

I remember when I came out...

"What?"

"When I came out," he repeated, as simple as discussing the weather. "When I told my parents I was gay. I knew I had to do it before college. I knew I had to be out *before* I went to college or I'd spend the next four years in the closet."

He was gay. He was telling me he was gay after discussing my divorce, which meant he knew *why* I got divorced.

I shook my head, really not sure what to say. "Yeah." I snorted in disbelief. "God forbid you end up living a lie until your fortieth birthday."

I didn't mean for it to sound so biting, but I didn't apologize.

He looked straight at me. I was half-expecting him to say sorry for bringing it up, for even discussing my personal life with me, but of course he didn't. "Is that what happened for you?" he asked me outright. "Did you get to forty and think—"

"I can't live a lie anymore," I finished for him.

He nodded. Then he did the darnedest thing. He put his hand on mine. "You're not living a lie anymore."

"No," I whispered. "I guess not."

He pulled back his hand, then he brightened considerably. "So? Seeing anyone?"

I shook my head and laughed at the incredulity of the conversation. "No."

Then he stood up off the stool, leaning in close to me as he did. "That's a shame," he said. He was close enough for me to feel the warmth of his skin, to smell his aftershave.

Fuck.

Still leaning in close to me, he slowly took my plate, then turned to walk around the counter and put the plates in the sink.

Apparently he spoke, but my head was still spinning at what had just happened, so I didn't hear him ask me anything. He waved his hand in front of my face to get my attention. "You okay?"

"Yeah," I replied, though the smug bastard smiled at me.

"I asked you how your coffee machine worked," he said.

I stood up, walked around the counter, and took the coffee from him, giving him a glare as I did. It didn't help that he smiled.

If it were Ryan speaking to me like that, I'd chip him for disrespecting me. Yet, I found it sassy in Cooper. The way his eyes danced, the way his lips twisted in that playful smirk.

The strong smell of coffee seemed to clear my senses a little, sobering me as I filled the machine, but when I turned to face Cooper again, he wasn't next to me. He was back at the dining table. And he was back to being all business.

I put his coffee in front of him, answering his questions, and discussing the insulation properties of different types of glazing and New York's planning requirements for retrofits. He was inquisitive and had a thirst for learning everything he could, and the way he just switched from flirting to professional left me wondering if I'd imagined the flirting side of it.

I mean, why *would* he flirt with me? Not only was I twice his age and the father of a friend of his, but it could be career-ending.

Well, not for me. I might get a slap on the wrist, but his career would be over before it had even begun.

Why *would* he flirt with me? Who the hell was I

kidding? What the hell was I thinking? I could have kicked myself for even considering the idea. First, the dream, then the fantasizing about it. Now this?

I needed to go out and hook up. Find some one-night stand and fuck him senseless. Or be fucked senseless. I needed to lose myself for just one night.

The fact that I'd fantasized about Cooper, about having him underneath me, should have been enough warning. It had been too long since I'd had sex. I was only interested in him, I told myself convincingly, because I'd gone too long without fulfilling sex.

I needed to go out. I needed to get laid. Then there'd be no more of this irresponsible infatuation with a twenty-two-year-old.

"Plans for tonight?" Cooper's voice startled me.

"Um, yeah," I mumbled. "I have plans." *Only very new, not-thought-through plans, But plans nonetheless.*

"Where are you off to?"

"Just catching up with an old friend." The truth was I had no clue.

"I'm supposed to be going out with Ryan and some other guys tonight. But I might cancel," he said, looking straight at me, as though he was trying to suggest something.

"You should go," I told him. "You don't need to be working here with me. Go hang out with the guys, have some fun."

Cooper stretched his arms above his head and yawned. He looked to the table in front of us and changed the subject. "We got a lot done today."

"We did," I agreed. "I have a bit more to catch up on tomorrow," I said, and he nodded. I quickly added, "You don't have to come in tomorrow. I won't tell Jennifer."

He smiled at that. "We'll see," he said. "But yeah, I should let you go. If you have plans."

I nodded. "I do."

Cooper started to pack his papers up. He closed down his laptop and slid it into his bag. "Thanks for lunch," he said. "Though, seriously? A peanut butter sandwich would have been fine."

He collected his things, and he'd no sooner walked out of the door than I was in the shower. *Fuck.* I had a hard-on from just being around him, his smile and his smell. It was the second time in as many days I needed to jerk off in the shower because the thought of him was too much.

It was the second time in as many days I imagined it was Cooper underneath me, over me, or his lips around me.

I didn't even wait for nightfall. I got dressed and went downtown to a local bar I'd been to plenty of times. It was only early, so there weren't many people, but everyone I looked at wasn't right for me.

I just wanted some faceless, nameless guy, who I could take to a hotel. I only lived a block away, but I never took casual hook-ups home. I wanted the anonymity, the security. But as I scoured the faces of men for hours, and as other men approached me, none of them were what I was looking for.

None of them had that shine in their eyes or that mischievous smile. None of them were young and vibrant, not like Cooper.

Fucking hell.

I ended up back at my apartment, pissed off and frustrated. I couldn't even have a one-night stand without thinking about him. I stripped down and climbed into bed naked, and this time, with images of him behind my eyelids when I jerked off, I imagined him inside me. I imagined what it would be like to be pinned underneath him, while he buried himself in me.

I came so hard my head spun.

But I slept like a baby.

———

THE NEXT MORNING I was up early, as always. Even being a Sunday didn't mean I couldn't get work done. Amazingly enough, for the first few hours I was up, I didn't think of Cooper at all.

Until it was about nine o'clock when my buzzer rang. Lionel's apologetic voice crackled through. "Sorry to interrupt you on a Sunday, sir."

"It's fine, Lionel."

"Cooper Jones is here again."

"Is he now?"

"Yes, sir," Lionel said. "He said to tell you he has coffee..." There was a muffle of voices again and Lionel groaned. "And peanut butter, sir. He said to tell you he bought you peanut butter."

I grinned into the intercom, grateful they couldn't see me smile. "Send him up."

CHAPTER FIVE

I UNLOCKED the door and waited, and true to his word, he walked in with two large coffees and a jar of peanut butter.

I was smiling at him. "What are you doing?"

"If you work, then I work," he said, handing me a coffee. "Jennifer's rules."

"I work every day."

"I don't mind," he said simply. "If I want to be the best, I need to do what the best does."

"Is that flattery?"

He lifted up the jar of peanut butter. "No, this is flattery," he said with a heart-stopping grin. "I can't believe you don't have any."

I smiled at him, and he stared at me. Neither of us spoke, and the air was electric. *Fuck.* "So, how was last night?" I asked, changing the subject and putting some distance between us.

"Oh, I never went," he said, sipping his coffee. "Wasn't up for it."

I was oddly relieved he hadn't gone out, hadn't picked

up anyone, or that he hadn't taken anyone home. Fuck, this was getting ridiculous.

Then he asked, "How was your night?"

"Uh, okay," I lied. "I was home pretty early."

"No hot date?" he asked lightly, but there was a seriousness in his eyes.

I shook my head. "No."

Cooper exhaled through puffed cheeks, seemingly relieved. "So, what's on the agenda for today?"

He was wearing jeans today, not suit pants. He had a button-down shirt, with his sleeves rolled up to his elbows, so I wasn't sure if he was here to work or not. It was definitely more relaxed.

"I, um, I'd like to get started on the Cariati file," I told him. I didn't exactly have anything for him to do but didn't want him to leave either.

This kid was messing with my head.

"Okay," he said, excited "You're doing the façades for that job, aren't you?"

"Yes."

"Can I watch?" he asked.

I stared at him disbelievingly. "You want to watch me draw?"

He nodded, but his cheeks tinted with embarrassment. "It's like watching a masterpiece from the beginning," he admitted quietly.

I couldn't help but smile. "Flattery will get you everywhere."

His eyebrows flickered. "Really?"

He stared at me until I had to look away. I put my coffee down on the counter, pretending to be distracted. Jesus. I wasn't imagining things. This kid was seriously flirting with me. *Fuck.*

I should have stopped it. I should have said no. I should have told him from the very beginning that this was a bad, bad idea.

But I couldn't. While the logical, sensible side of my brain was telling me to put an end right now to this nonsense, the selfish, infatuated, stupid part of my brain wanted it.

My body wanted it.

I glanced back at him, at his smug little smile, then snatched the jar of peanut butter from his hand. I looked at the jar and turned it over in my hands. "Flattery in a jar, huh?"

He smiled as he sipped his coffee, then assessed the dining table. "So, are we working today?"

Work. Right. "Yes, we are," I said, getting my brain back on track. "You can keep going with the specs on the Lewington job while I get started. It takes a while to grid it all out."

"I can't believe you really start each job by drawing it out," he said, walking over to the table. "You know it's the twenty-first century, right? We have computers now."

"I like to see it develop in front of me," I tried to explain. "If I draw it out, it seems to give me a better feel for the overall tone. I've spoken to the Cariatis many times. I know what they want. I can see it in my head, and it comes out better by my hand than with a computer."

I looked up then, to find Cooper staring at me. He was smiling as if some errant thought made him happy. "That's amazing," he said. Then he added quietly, "You're amazing."

I was taken aback by his blatant compliment, pleased, but a little embarrassed. I looked at the table instead of him. "Oh. I'm not sure about that."

"I am," he said confidently. "And there wasn't even any peanut butter involved."

It made me laugh, and as I sat down, I opened my grid pad and pulled my drafting leads from my briefcase. Cooper looked at the specialized pencils. "Do they still make those?"

I rolled my eyes. "It's not a quill and inkwell, you know."

He laughed. "No, in the museum they have the quills and drafting leads in separate displays."

I chuckled, despite his constant jibes at my age. "Comments like that counteract the peanut butter."

He grinned, and instead of looking even slightly remorseful, he looked at me like I'd just proposed a challenge.

I tapped the table with my index finger. "Enough with the smart-ass comments. Work."

Like I hadn't spoken at all, he said, "How about we have a little bet?"

"Pardon?" I asked. "As in a wager?"

"More of a professional social experiment," he mused. "How about, for the next four hours, you do your drawing of the façade and I enter in the exterior details into the CAD program? At the end of the four hours, we'll see, one, who was more productive, and two, who was more accurate." He opened his laptop and looked at me expectantly.

"And what exactly is the wager?"

"The loser buys lunch."

I smiled at him, at the gleam in his eyes, and at the daring of his smile. "Deal."

I slid the spec sheet across the table to Cooper. "You'll need that," I told him and started with my grid paper and went by memory alone. It was a remodeling job on an old building, strictly confined by city building codes.

I knew those codes like the back of my hand, I knew what the owners wanted, and I knew how to make it happen. So, picking up one of my drafting leads, I got started, and not even the annoying *tap-tap-tap* of Cooper on his laptop keyboard could distract me.

It was my favorite part of my job. Of course, all jobs went through the specifically designed CAD program, but for me, this was where each job started.

It was about two hours later that Cooper stood up and stretched. He walked off toward the kitchen and came back with the jar of peanut butter and a spoon. "What?" he asked when I looked at him. "It was my jar of flattery."

He then proceeded to eat it by the spoonful, and one time I looked up at him, he was concentrating hard on the computer screen with the spoon still in his mouth. It was... cute.

Soon after that, my stomach let me know when it was lunchtime, and sure enough, when I checked the time, it had almost been four hours. I stood up and walked into the kitchen, grabbed two bottled waters and a spoon, and went back to the table. I put the two waters down, leaned my ass against the edge of the table near Cooper, and picked up the jar of peanut butter.

"How are you doing with your wager?" I asked as I scooped out a spoonful from the jar.

He sighed. "Well, I'm done, but I know it won't be as good as yours."

I stuck the spoon in my mouth, and as soon as I tasted the peanut butter, I couldn't help but groan. "This is good."

Cooper looked up at me, seemingly transfixed by the spoon in my mouth. "Told you," he said a little gruffly. He shook his head and looked quickly back to his laptop, turning it around to face me. "Not that we really even need to check because I'm sure yours will put mine to shame."

I looked at the screen. "You've done a really good job," I told him. "The façade looks good; the elevations are clean. It looks good."

"Mmm," he said, not convinced.

"You've got the coding correct," I reassured him. "And considering it's a new program to you, don't dismiss that. You've done a great job."

"Righto," he mumbled. "Let's have a look at yours." He stood up, walked around to my side of the table, and picked up my grid pad. He was quiet for a long moment, so I walked around and stood beside him. "Jesus," he whispered. "It's... this is amazing."

I smiled at him, and he shook his head.

"The shading, the perspective, the lines..." He seemed lost for words. "Wow. It's um, it's..."

"It's lunchtime and you're paying," I told him, taking the pad and throwing it onto the table. Cooper grinned at me for a beat too long, walked to my front door, and held it open for me.

"No jokes about the elderly?" I asked as we got to the elevator. "Yesterday you were full of cheek about my age."

"Can you remember yesterday?" he asked, wide-eyed. "Your medication must really work."

I pressed the button for the lobby. "You're such a little shit."

I thought I might offend him by calling him that. But by the way he grinned proudly, I doubted I could offend him if I tried.

The streets of New York on a Sunday were still busy, only people dressed a little more casually than they did during the week. We started to walk and ended up near the park at a vendor. Cooper stared at me. "I might be a lowly intern, but I can afford more than a pretzel for lunch."

I laughed at him. "I happen to like these." So two pretzels later, we found a bench seat and started to eat our lunch.

Cooper was thoughtful as he ate, looking around. "I love this city," he said.

"Me too." I smiled when I looked at him. "It has a hum, an energy, doesn't it?"

He nodded. "Yeah, it does. But"—then he shrugged—"you'll probably think I'm crazy, but you wanna know what I love about New York City?" He shook his head like he couldn't believe he was about to admit something. "I love the skyscrapers. I love the glass and steel. I love the purpose this city has. I love how the new buildings integrate with the old ones. I love the history and the modern. I mean some of these buildings are works of art…"

I stared at him, and he stopped talking and blushed, ducking his head. "See? Told you you'd think I was crazy."

I shook my head slowly. "I love that too," I said quietly. "Everything you said, that's what I love about it too." I shook my head, a little perplexed that this man, this man half my age, understood me.

Cooper smiled and looked down at the half-eaten pretzel in his hand. "I've never told anyone that."

I laughed nervously. "I've told people, but they've never really understood me."

He looked at me then, and neither one of us spoke. I just stared at him—wondering what on earth it was about him that intrigued me so much—and right there, in a city of millions with the noise of people and cars and buzzing past us, we sat in silence and had ourselves a moment.

He looked back down at his hands, with tinted cheeks, and exhaled as though looking at me had rendered him unable to breathe.

I liked that more than I should. "Come on," I said, standing up. "I want to show you something."

He stood up, threw the rest of his lunch in the bin, and looked at me with bright eyes. "What is it?"

"This way," I said, walking in a different direction than the way we'd come. Two blocks over, I pointed up. "See that?" It was a nondescript commercial building, dwarfed by the taller buildings beside it. Usually overlooked by passersby, it wasn't the biggest or the grandest, but it was a classic building that any decent architect would appreciate for its subtlety.

"The Crawson building?"

I nodded. "I did that."

Cooper's eyes widened. "Really? I mean, I'm not doubting you... it's just... wow."

I laughed. "Yes, really. Complete retrofit. Exterior façade to replicate the existing, even enhance the history of the building, but its interior is something else. You should see it. It's classic art-deco design but completely sustainable." I showed him the cubic forms, the strong sense of lines, the sleek curving forms, and illusion of pillars.

When I finally stopped talking, I looked at Cooper to find he wasn't even looking at the building. He was staring at me. "Can you show me?"

"Inside the building?"

He shook his head. "No, show me how you draw. I want to be able to do that."

"Oh."

"Will you show me? I want to learn. I want to see things how you see them."

I looked at him again, and he stared straight back at me. His eyes never faltered, never strayed from mine. All I could do was nod. "Yes."

He smiled magnificently. "No time like the present."

We started to walk back to my apartment. "Are you sure you don't have anywhere else you'd rather be?" I asked. "Working with me on a Sunday is hardly anyone's idea of fun."

"Well, I'm not anyone," he said brightly. "I happen to enjoy it."

"I'm glad you do," I replied.

The rest of the walk back to my place was quiet, but as soon as we were inside, he pulled his chair next to mine at the table. "So where do we start?"

He had the basic, graphic art and technical drawing skills all architecture kids had. He admitted to that—he could draw a building easily enough. But he couldn't draw it to life, he said. Not like me.

So for the next few hours, we sat side by side at my table with my grid pad and pencils. Sometimes our knees bumped, sometimes our thighs were completely touching, sometimes he'd rest his arm on the back of my chair, some- times our hands would be so close they'd almost be touching.

And we talked, and we laughed, and we told stories, and he smelled so good. But he listened, and he studied, and he copied, and it was pretty obvious this kid had talent.

It was also pretty obvious there was something between us. I wasn't imagining it. I'd catch him staring at me, or sometimes his breath would catch, and every now and then when our hands touched, it'd make my heart rate take off and my mouth would go dry.

Sometimes I'd catch myself staring at him. I was lost in

his brown hair and hazel eyes and kissable, pink lips. When he was concentrating, or lost in thought at the drawing in front of him, I'd have to *make* myself look away.

When he turned to ask me about something, our faces were so close, within leaning distance. His question was long forgotten, and his hazel eyes darkened as he stared at me. He licked his lips and leaned in just a fraction.

He was going to kiss me. And I wanted to. I wanted to feel his lips. I wanted to taste him, touch him, and it was that want that made me panic.

I shot out of my seat and went into the kitchen, shaking my head of the Cooper-daze it was apparently in, and tried to calm my hammering heart.

I turned to watch Cooper stand up slowly. "I should probably go," he said quietly.

"Okay," I said, out of breath.

His brow furrowed and he collected his laptop and stuffed it into his bag. He exhaled through puffed-out cheeks and mumbled something about seeing himself out. Unable to do much else, I nodded, compliantly.

He walked out of my apartment, and not three seconds later, there was a knock on the door. Knowing who it would be, I looked through the peephole anyway and nervously ran my hands through my hair before opening the door.

Cooper looked rattled, confused even, so I asked, "Everything okay?"

He stared at me for a long second, then blurted out, "I think we should kiss."

CHAPTER SIX

"YOU WHAT?"

"I think we should kiss," he repeated, clearly flustered. "We should just do it and get it out of the way. Then we can forget about it and get over it, move on, clear the air, whatever. But it's just always there," he said, almost pacing in my doorway. "It's right there between us, and it's driving me crazy I can't concentrate. All I can think about is what the fuck kissing you would feel like, or taste like."

My heart was hammering and my stomach was in knots. He was standing right in front of me, telling me he wanted to kiss me.

"I'm not concerned about work," he went on to say. "Because I'm sure, I'm *absolutely certain* that if I just kiss you once and get it out of my system, I'll be fine. I'll be back to normal, and we can just act like nothing happened. I know you want to kiss me too," he said, still ranting. "I can see it when you look at me. You stare at my mouth and you lick your lips, and it's like you're trying to not want to kiss me, and I don't blame you because it's weird. I get that. But I think if we just did it and got it out of the way, we could work together without all this wondering about what you might taste like..." His eyes went wide and he paled. The look on my face must have scared him. "Or not," he mumbled, taking a step back from me. "I've obviously misread the signs and you're not saying anything and I've just ruined everything." He turned and almost ran for the elevator.

"Cooper, stop," I said, following him and grabbing his arm. "You haven't misread anything."

He exhaled in a rush, pure relief, and ran his hand through his hair.

"But I'm not sure," I said, taking a step closer to him so we were almost touching.

"We don't have to," he said quickly. "I shouldn't have suggested—"

His words died when I slid my hand along his jaw. I leaned in and could feel his warm breath on my lips. "I'm not sure if once would be enough."

His eyes were wide and he licked his lips. "Probably not."

Our lips met, open and soft. It was a tender and wary kiss, scared of what was happening, of where this was going. Neither of us moved for a long second, but I gently pulled his bottom lip between mine, and he gasped.

It seemed to kick him into gear because he let his bag fall to the floor so he could use two hands to hold me. His lips opened as he deepened the kiss, sliding his arms around my waist as his tongue slid into my mouth.

I groaned. Or maybe it was him.

I held his face as we kissed, taking in everything about him—the warmth of his body, his soft lips, his taste, his smell. He made my head spin and my knees weak, my heart was thumping, and I wanted more.

But then the elevator arrived at our floor, and before the door could open, I pulled Cooper's hand, leading him back into my apartment. He grabbed his bag off the floor and made it inside just as old Mrs. Giordano walked out of the elevator. I gave her a polite wave and smile as I closed the door, and Cooper burst out laughing.

I leaned against the closed door and grinned at him. "Mrs. Giordano doesn't need to see that."

Cooper put his bag down against the wall near the door, smiling breathlessly. "Mrs. whats-her-name might like to see it."

"Mrs. Giordano is ninety-two years old," I told him. I was still leaning against the door, and he was right in front of me. He wasn't pressed up against me, but he wasn't letting me move either. His gaze was flickering from my eyes to my mouth, as though he was about to kiss me again. My voice was just a whisper. "I thought you said just one kiss?"

"I thought you said it wouldn't be enough," he whispered back as he pressed his lips to mine again. He held my face this time, as he opened my mouth with his own. Our tongues met, and he pressed his body to mine.

I wrapped my hands around his back and pulled him tighter against me. I couldn't help it. I didn't want to want him. I didn't want to like it. I didn't want to need it.

But I did.

He slowed the kiss, dragging his lips from mine, looking down until his forehead rested on my cheek, then my chin, and eventually he took a small step back. He was breathing hard, but he was smiling. My hands were still on his hips, so he took another small step back, stepping away from me. "I think I should go now," he said.

I worried he might panic at the realization of what had

just happened. We had just kissed. Twice. Me, his friend's father, a man twice his age. His boss.

"There's no need to panic," I said, realizing how stupid it sounded as soon as I'd said it.

"Oh, I'm not panicking," he said gruffly. Then he very obviously readjusted the bulge in his jeans.

"Oh."

Cooper laughed, embarrassed. He took a deep breath and exhaled slowly, then looked me in the eye. His eyes were bright and playful. "I will see you in the morning at the office."

"Okay," I answered, trying to gauge his mood.

He picked up his bag, put his hand on the door handle, and said, "I'm going to need you to move from the door."

"Oh," I said, stepping around him. "Sure."

Then he stepped right up close and pecked my lips again, kissing me for the third time.

"That's three," I told him.

He opened the door. "I'm not counting," he said as he walked toward the elevator. He looked around and smiled at me before he stepped in.

I closed the door to my apartment, wondering what the fuck I'd just done.

I'd just crossed every professional and personal line I'd ever had. He worked for me, and he was my son's friend. Meaning, he wasn't just someone Ryan knew, he was someone Ryan had gone to school with. As in the same age. As in exactly *half* my age. I tried not to think about that. Or what that meant.

Cooper was an adult. A very willing, consenting adult. A very well-endowed adult by what I'd felt pressed against my hip.

And with that thought, I stripped off and got in the

shower, seeking relief. Again. To images of Cooper. *Again.* What he would look like underneath me with his head thrown back or on his knees with his lips around me.

The lips I'd just tasted.

Fuck.

I came so hard the room spun. I leaned against the tiles in the shower to catch my breath and until I was pretty sure I could stand without falling.

Fuck, this guy was messing with my head.

I thought about him all night, what he'd say in the morning at the office, how he'd react when he saw me. I went to bed thinking about him. I dreamed of him. I needed to jerk off again in the morning.

It was getting ridiculous.

It was with a dreaded anticipation I went to work the next day. An errant thought occurred to me when I was stepping out of the elevator to my office that he could report me for sexual harassment, and in that split-second, a thousand thoughts ran through my head.

I half expected Jennifer to tell me I had a team of lawyers sitting in my office, but she just smiled and handed me messages. "Coffee is on your desk."

I ran my hand through my hair and huffed out a breath in relief. Jesus, what had I gotten myself into?

I was at my desk about a half an hour later when Jennifer walked in with Cooper behind her. He was dressed in his usual tailor-fitted suit, looking even better today than he ever had, but he said nothing more than a polite and quiet, "Good morning, Mr. Elkin."

I had a lunch meeting and a consultants meeting, and I saw him briefly throughout the day. But not once did he make eye contact. He didn't look at me and smile or laugh like I was used to seeing.

He basically didn't acknowledge me. He was professional and stoic, like nothing had happened between us. Maybe he was right. Maybe if he kissed me once, he would get it out of his system and move on like nothing happened at all.

I, on the other hand, was a distracted mess.

I didn't know if he was playing some kind of game. I didn't know if he was just being professional or if I was truly out of his system and now meant nothing to him.

All day, every time the phone rang, I half expected Jennifer to tell me one of the partners wanted to see me because a complaint had been lodged against me.

That call never came, of course, but at six o'clock when Jennifer knocked on my door to say goodnight, Cooper was behind her. I looked up from my desk. "Goodnight, Jennifer," I said. Then I looked back at the papers on my desk. "Mr. Jones. A moment, please."

Jennifer gave a nod and left Cooper to walk in. He sat down and looked around my office, then at me. "Yes?"

I didn't exactly know what to say or how to say it. So I went with a safer, "You've been busy today?"

He looked at me seriously and said, "It's technically after hours, so can I speak freely?"

I looked at him, unsure of what he meant. "Yes."

But he didn't speak. He threw his head back and laughed. "Jennifer has been on my ass all day," he said with a laugh. "Said you looked stressed this morning and didn't need any interruptions from the likes of me."

"The likes of you?"

"Those were her words."

I smiled, relieved, and exhaled loudly. "I almost had a panic attack getting out of the elevator this morning," I admitted. "I wondered if my boss and his lawyers would be in my office when I got here."

Cooper's smile died. "What for?"

"A sexual harassment case from a certain twenty-two-year-old employee," I said, looking pointedly at him.

I could have compiled a list of how I expected him to react, but laughter wouldn't have been on it. He burst out laughing, and when he looked at me again and saw the look on my face, he laughed some more.

"It's hardly funny," I said, rolling my eyes.

"Were you really worried?" he asked, still smiling.

"I didn't know what to think."

"Neither did I," he admitted. "So, is this where you tell me it was just the one kiss and nothing more? Is that what you called me in here for? To say thanks but no thanks?"

"It was actually three kisses."

"I wasn't counting."

I sighed and ran my fingers through my hair. This was it. This was where the line got drawn or where the lines got blurred.

"You seemed pretty into it from where I was standing," he said.

I barked out a laugh. He had no idea how into it I was, how often I thought of him or the positions I thought of him in. *Fuck.*

I had to be losing my mind.

"What do you want?" I asked, trying to take the pressure off making it my decision.

"I want an honest answer."

I exhaled in a huff. He wasn't letting me out of this. "I... I, um..."

"Oh, for fuck's sake," he said impatiently. "If I were to

offer to bring dinner to your place tonight, would you say yes or no?"

"Are you always so forthright?" I asked. "Or is it a Gen Y thing?"

"You mean Millennial?"

"I prefer Gen Y."

He snorted. "So, dinner?"

I wanted to. God, I wanted to. But...

He raised one eyebrow and studied me for a long moment. "For one of the best, most sought-after draftsmen in the industry, you're not very good at making decisions."

"Professional decisions are easy. Personal ones are not."

"Oh, Tom, just answer the question."

He'd called me Tom. Not sir, not Mr. Elkin, not even Thomas. He'd called me Tom.

"Yes. Yes, I want dinner. Yes, I want more. Once wasn't enough," I blurted out. "Once was never going to be enough."

He grinned at me and held up three fingers. "It was actually three kisses."

I bit back a sigh. "Are you always so infuriating?"

Cooper laughed. "Yep, it's a Mill" he caught himself. "It's a Gen Y thing."

I groaned. "Can I take back the offer of dinner?"

"Nope," he said, standing up. "I'm getting Chinese food, and I'll be at your place in"—he looked at his watch —"half an hour."

I smiled as I watched him walk out. When the door closed behind him, I let out a groan and ran my hands through my hair. I shut down my laptop, picked up my briefcase, and turned the lights off when I left.

I think I grinned the whole way home.

CHAPTER SEVEN

THE AIR between us was electric as we ate dinner. And the more I tried to ignore it, the worse it seemed to get. It was all suggestive glances, shy blushes, and licking lips. I stared as he took food from his chopsticks, as he opened his mouth and chewed. And he seemed transfixed by my hands.

It was... intoxicating.

When the food was all but gone, I stood up to clear the table and offered him another glass of wine. He took the refilled glass, then stood beside me, leaning his ass against the table. He was still wearing his suit pants, the first two buttons of his business shirt were undone, and his tie was gone. His eyes were bright and his lips were in a smug little smirk. My heart was hammering, yet he seemed completely at ease.

"You make me nervous," I admitted.

He looked at me. "You? The great Thomas Elkin nervous?"

I chuckled. "Well, here I'm just Tom."

"Well, Tom," he said, taking my wine glass and putting it on the table. "I think you should kiss me now."

"Really?" I asked. His confidence was mesmerizing.

He licked his lips and nodded. So I leaned across and brushed his lips with mine. It was soft and sweet, but then he moved to deepen the kiss. I moved from beside him to stand in front of him and pressed my body against his as I opened my mouth for him.

This was a different kind of kiss.

The first time we'd kissed had been just a kiss. But this was going somewhere.

I slid one arm around his back and kept one hand around his neck as I kissed him, a mass of tongues, lips, mouths, and moans. Cooper raked his hands around my back and down, over my ass. He pulled me against him so I could feel him. All of him.

Fuck.

He was hard and so was I. I knew he could feel it. There was no way he couldn't feel my cock against his through the fabric of our pants.

Then he was pulling up my shirt and slipping his fingers under the waistband. Before I could pull my mouth from his to ask what he was doing, he'd undone my zipper and palmed my cock through my briefs.

"Cooper," I started. I wanted to tell him that it wasn't a good idea, but it felt so good. So, so good.

So I undid the button and zipper on his pants and slid my hand over his briefs, wrapping my hand around him the best I could through the fabric.

He moaned so loud, I almost came.

"Fuck," he gasped, and he gripped me harder, pulling, rubbing, squeezing. I did the same to him, and he bucked into me, only this time he shuddered and his head fell back as he thrust into my fist.

Watching him come, feeling him in my hand, brought me undone.

His hand gripped me as I erupted between us. I all but fell into him, collapsing with the force of my orgasm, and he seemed to convulse with aftershocks. When the room had stopped spinning, I realized his face was buried in my neck.

He chuckled. "Well, that's dessert."

I laughed and peeled myself off him. We were a sticky mess. "We need to shower."

He toed off his shoes right there. I hadn't actually meant that we'd shower together, but he took my hand and said, "Where's the bathroom?" He walked toward the hall.

"Last door on the right." It was my bedroom, which I think surprised him. He looked at the bed, then at me, and he grinned.

"Bathroom," I said, pointing to the door. He still had hold of my hand.

He led the way, smiling as he undid the buttons on my shirt, and as I slid his pants over his hips and as my shirt fell from my shoulders, I knew this was it.

Despite what we'd just done in the dining room, we were about to be naked together. I was forty-four, he was twenty-two. This was where the difference between us would be really evident.

I had a spattering of hair on my chest that was graying, like the hair on my head, and while I worked out, my body was... well, it was forty-four years old. Whereas Cooper's body was taut and trim, his chest was hairless, though he had a light trail of brown hair from his navel to his heavily hung, uncut dick.

He turned to start the water while I took off my socks. He washed the cum from his stomach first, then turned around and put his head under, closing his eyes. "You getting in?"

I followed him into the shower, and taking the soap, I ran it over his body. He smiled, then moved from under the spray of water to let me in. I washed the mess from my stomach, and when I turned to put my head under, Cooper put his hands on my chest.

"Mmm," he hummed as he ran his fingers through my chest hair. "I like this." Then he snaked his hand down lower and cupped my balls. "I like this, too."

I couldn't help but chuckle but swatted his hand away. "Are you always so forthright?"

"Yep," he said with a smile. "It's a Gen Y thing, remember?"

I rolled my eyes, so he took his own dick in his hand and gave it a stroke. He was half hard again already.

"Is that a Gen Y thing?" I asked.

He smirked. "That's a twenty-two-year-old-in-the-shower-with-a-hot-guy thing. I can't help it. You're hot and I'm horny."

I laughed out loud, turned the shower off and handed him a towel. "Um, I'll find you some clean clothes," I told him. "I'll send ours to be dry-cleaned."

I wrapped my towel around me and walked from the en-suite to the walk-in closet. I pulled on a pair of jeans and took out a pair of cargo shorts and a T-shirt for him.

He was standing in my room with only a towel around his waist, looking at my king-sized bed. "Looks comfy," he said with a grin.

Ignoring his comment, I threw the clean clothes at him. "I'll organize the dry-cleaning."

I picked up our soiled suits and shirts from the bath-room floor, and when I walked back into my bedroom,

Cooper was pulling up the cargos. He was smiling at me as he shoved his half-hard cock into the pants. "No underwear, Tom? Is it for easy access later?"

I tried not to smile at him, but my belly tightened at the thought. "You're incorrigible."

He laughed, and I left him there. I bagged the clothes and called reception just as Cooper came out of my room. He looked me up and down. "How come I have a shirt but you don't?" he asked, but it was more of a rhetorical question. "Not that I mind." Then he walked into the kitchen and opened the fridge. "Want a water?"

"Make yourself at home," I said sarcastically, though I kind of liked it that he felt comfortable here.

He handed me a bottle of water anyway and walked out onto the balcony. "Oh my God."

I followed him out to find him staring at the view. New York City at its finest—tall gray buildings, narrow roads with yellow cabs sidelined by green trees that led to the enormity that was Central Park.

I smiled at the look on his face. "This apartment is pretty central."

"Pretty central?" he asked. "It's right *on* Central."

I laughed. "Not quite. But close."

He shook his head, then turned back to look up the street at the Empire State Building. New York City lights at night were something special. "How do you not live out here on your balcony with that view? I mean, I've seen it during the day from here, but at night..."

"It's amazing, isn't it?"

He nodded, taking in and pointing out certain landmarks and the buildings he recognized. After a while, I started to get cool, so I went inside and came back out with a shirt on. Cooper sighed. "The view was much better without the shirt."

I smiled at his words but changed the subject. "Dry-cleaning said they'd be a few hours," I told him. "You can wear those clothes home if you like."

Cooper shrugged. "I don't mind. I can wait, but if I happen to fall asleep in that big comfy bed of yours, I won't mind that either."

I wanted to tell him I didn't think that was a good idea, that that would be moving too fast. I looked at him and couldn't seem to find the words.

CHAPTER EIGHT

COOPER DIDN'T STAY the night. But he did stay till midnight, took his freshly dry-cleaned suit, kissed me in the doorway, and left.

At work, he was ever the professional. Never granting me more than a polite "Good morning, Mr. Elkin." And he diligently did his job.

He was exceptionally good at his job.

As one of the senior partners, I had a slew of architects under me, who were delegated a range of jobs. So while yes, I had chosen him to work on my team, he was one of many. And it wouldn't have been unusual for me not to see him every day.

But I looked for him. I kept an eye on him, and I watched what he did. But I didn't speak to him, not more than a hello or a courteous nod in the hall.

He was really very good at his job. He was also very good at pretending he didn't know me.

But on the Thursday—four days since I'd seen him outside work—just before closing time, Jennifer's intercom buzzed. "Yes, Jennifer?"

"Did you call for Mr. Jones?" she asked. "He says you asked to see him."

I smiled. "Yes, I did. Please send him in."

The door opened and in he walked, wearing his suit pants, shirt, tie, and a vest, no jacket. He looked... hot.

He sat down across from me and smiled. "You wanted to see me?"

"Did I?"

"Yeah, I'm pretty sure you did," he said with a nod. "I'm sure you had work that needed to be done tonight. At your place."

I smiled at him. "Oh, yes. Now I remember."

He looked like the cat that got the canary. "And it's your turn to buy dinner," he added. "Not that I'd ever tell you what to order, but I feel like pizza."

I couldn't help but chuckle. "God forbid you tell me what to do."

He stood up. "Half an hour?"

"See you then."

"Pepperoni and peppers."

"I thought you weren't telling me what to do."

"It's a Gen Y thing," he said before he opened the door and walked out.

I was still smiling when Jennifer walked in. "Anything you need me to do before I leave, Mr. Elkin?"

"No, I won't be far behind you," I told her. "I'll be working from home tonight."

"Can I order you something to eat?" she asked.

"No, I've got it covered. Thank you."

"Very well. I'll see you tomorrow," she said. "Don't work too hard."

I smiled at her as she walked out, knowing not much work would be getting done tonight. And thirty minutes later, I was home and pizza was ordered, when the doorman buzzed. "Yes, Lionel?"

"Sir, Mr. Jones is here."

"Send him up."

I unlocked the door, took out two beers from the fridge, and smiled when there was a knock. "Come in."

Still wearing the suit and vest he'd worn that day, Cooper walked in to find me in the kitchen. He took the offered beer and didn't hesitate to kiss me. It was a slow, deliberate peck on the lips that made my stomach knot—a kiss that promised more to come.

Then he said, "I don't think Lionel likes me."

"Why?"

"He won't let me come straight up," he said, almost petulantly. "It's like I have to check in with him first."

I took a swig of my beer to hide my smile. "He's doing his job."

"But I've been here like five times, and he's seen us walk in and out together, and he still stops me," he added. "What's it gonna take for him to be cool with it?"

Cool with it? Dear God, he really was twenty-two. "He'll be *cool* with it when I tell him you can come and go as you please."

"What, like I live here or something?"

"Yes, like you live here or something. And you don't live here, and you're not my *something*."

He understood then what I meant. "Oh." He looked down at his beer. "Fair enough."

I lifted his chin and stood in front of him. "Telling Lionel you have access is like my equivalent of giving you a key to my house."

"Yeah, I get it."

I kissed him softly. "I didn't mean you weren't something to me."

His eyes widened and he looked at me squarely. "What am I to you?"

"Mesmerizing. Confounding. Amusing."

He smiled slowly. "They're some pretty good adjectives."

I kissed him softly again. "Yes, that's it. You're some pretty good adjectives to me."

There was a loud knock on the door. "Pizza."

Cooper's eyes narrowed. "He lets the *pizza guy* come up without buzzing?"

I laughed and went to the door, and when I came back, Cooper was looking at the intercom, finger raised. "Which button do I press?" he mumbled to himself. He didn't wait for an answer; he just pressed the first button.

Lionel answered. "Yes, Mr. Elkin?"

"You let the pizza guy up and not me?" Cooper said into the intercom.

"Mr. Elkin, is everything okay?" Lionel sounded alarmed.

I swatted Cooper's hand away and pressed the button. "Yes, Lionel, I'm fine. Mr. Jones here is feeling a little unloved."

"Am I to alert you when Mr. Jones arrives, sir?"

I looked Cooper up and down, finally landing on his face. "Yes, you can still let me know when Mr. Jones arrives," I said, and Cooper's mouth fell open. "For now."

"Very well, Mr. Elkin," Lionel said through the intercom.

I released the button and put the pizzas on the counter. Cooper glared at me.

I smiled at him. "You're cute when you pout."

He huffed. "I think I'll need a lot more adjectives from you yet."

I turned the pizza box to face him and opened it. "Hungry, cute."

"You said that one already."

"Impatient, talented, conceited, smug."

"They're similes. Didn't they teach you similes in school back in the olden days?"

"Smartass, juvenile, petulant, belligerent…"

Cooper picked up a slice of pizza, bit into it, and chewed thoughtfully. He swallowed his food and said, "Mmm, well, I like talented and conceited, but smart-ass and juvenile were a little harsh. I think we might need to go back to cute."

I shook my head and sighed. "Okay, you're a cute, belligerent little shit. How was that?"

He took another bite of his pizza and spoke with his mouth full, "Much better."

I gave up. I doubted I'd ever win. I took a slice of pizza, and he clinked his beer bottle to mine and gave me a cheeky grin.

"So do you really think I'm cute?"

"Just shut up and eat your pizza."

Cooper gave me that smug little smile then told me all about his week so far. How he'd been busy with the team getting basics done and learning what he could. It was easy to see that he loved it, how animated he got, how it seemed he could talk for hours about projects and buildings and drawings and concepts.

Even long after the pizza was gone and we'd been on the sofa for a while, we were still discussing design theories and building codes and planning laws. It amazed me that he could make me smile with just a pout one minute, then be a professional adult whom I could talk to for hours the next.

Then he changed the subject. "I'm sorry if telling Jennifer you asked to see me was out of line," he said. "But I figured if I didn't, I wouldn't get to see you."

"It's fine," I told him. "I'm glad you did."

He smiled. "Me too." Then he slid himself across the sofa and kissed me. But he didn't stop there. He slowly leaned backward, pulling me with him, so I was lying over him. He only stopped kissing me so he could maneuver himself into a better position for me to settle between his legs, then his mouth was on mine again.

Cooper opened his legs wider and held onto me tighter, and I rocked a little on top of him while we kissed. But it was languid and soft; there was no hot and heavy desire. His eyes closed gently, sleepily. When I brushed his hair from his forehead, I saw my watch. It was after one, we'd been talking for hours, and I'd completely lost track of time.

"Come on, sleepyhead," I said, getting off him, pulling him to his feet. "It's too late for you to go home. You can stay here."

I led him down the hall toward the spare room, Ryan's room, but he turned straight into my bedroom and started to strip off. He threw his suit pants over the chair and climbed into my bed in his underwear.

Into my side of the bed.

I stood there, not sure what to do. I contemplated arguing but realized arguing with Cooper was futile. So instead, I went back out to the living room, turned off the lights, and by the time I'd changed into pajama pants and got into bed, Cooper was sound asleep.

WAKING up to the feeling of being watched isn't particularly pleasant. A sleep-rumpled Cooper looked at me apologetically. "I guess this could be awkward," he said. "I mean, if we let it be awkward. But I'm all for thinking fuck it, let's *not* be awkward. Let's have pancakes for breakfast and then when you're covered in maple syrup, we can shower together, or I can lick you clean. Whichever you prefer."

I smiled. "Good morning, Cooper."

"Morning, Tom," he said with a grin. "So, pancakes?"

I looked at the alarm clock and fell back with a groan. Six a.m. "Pancakes."

He bounced up on the bed, still wearing only his briefs. I could see the heavy outline of his morning wood. He knew I saw, he made no attempt to hide it. In fact, he then walked to the kitchen and proceeded to make pancakes, still only wearing his briefs.

Needless to say, breakfast was a mess, there was a lot of licking, followed by a hot shower where Cooper dropped to his knees and took my hardened cock into his mouth.

I returned the favor on my bed, where he arched his back, gripped the sheets, and screamed as he shot hard down my throat. He then chuckled and writhed on my bed until his body recovered while I took a shirt from my wardrobe and laid it on the bed next to him. "You'll have to wear the suit pants you wore yesterday to work, but at least people won't know you didn't go home if you're wearing a new shirt."

Cooper laughed. "It wouldn't have been the first time I've done the walk of shame."

I rolled my eyes at him. "Come on, you need to get up. Don't want to be late."

He stretched lazily and grinned, his spent cock lying heavy across his hip. "I don't know, I think the boss might be in a particularly good mood this morning." Then he added, "Anyway, I think he likes me."

I did up the fly on my pants, not game to look at him in case he saw that exact truth on my face. "Whatever gives you that idea?"

"The way he gripped my hair and moaned my name in the shower."

I blushed. The little shit made me blush. I cleared my throat. "Right, I better go clean up this kitchen."

FOR THE NEXT TWO WEEKS, we fooled around. Usually at my place, though I went to his apartment on the second weekend. It was small, very small, but clean... and small. *Did I mention it was small?* But it was close enough to the office, and he seemed to like it. Compared to my place, it was at the other end of the spectrum of places to live.

So, at his place or mine, we spent time together. Lost in long conversations or long make-out sessions, I couldn't seem to get enough of him, and as baffling as it was to me, it seemed he couldn't get enough of me either.

But we never had sex. Well, not intercourse-sex. We were close a few times, and it was something we clearly both wanted, but it was something we never discussed. Like it was a step we were too scared to take.

At work, he was always the professional. He kept his cool, though I noticed that smug little smirk every now and then, but to anyone else, from what I could tell, no one suspected a thing.

It was Thursday afternoon and Jennifer's intercom buzzed. "Mr. Jones is here to see you."

"Thank you," I replied.

He walked in with some drafting papers and sat down across from me.

I looked at the plans he was holding. "What are they?"

"Props," he answered. "For Jennifer's sake. I had to come in here with something."

I chuckled at him. "To what do I owe the pleasure?"

"Well," he started, and he seemed nervous. "I know I said I'd come over tonight, but the guys are going out later and they asked me to join them. It's been a while..."

I looked at him, a little confused. "Cooper, that's fine. You don't need my permission. You're young; you should go out."

"It's with Ryan."

Oh.

"That's fine," I lied. He was young. He should go out and enjoy his life. Not be stuck at home with some old man like me.

"You can't lie for shit," he said flatly. "And I know what you're thinking. Just because I'm young and we don't go out doesn't mean I don't enjoy spending time with you." He stared straight at me, seeing right through me.

"We should go out more," I admitted.

"No, we shouldn't," he replied. "We can't and you know it." He looked around my office before looking back at me. "And that's okay, Tom. I like what we do. But I'd like to go out with the boys tonight."

"Of course," I said with a smile. "That means I don't have to listen to your shit music tonight."

He smirked as he stood up to leave. "No, you can listen to your Hits of the Eighties crap without me."

I opted for some classical music instead, knowing Cooper would hate it, and spent the night going over some concept budgets. It was quiet and lovely, but something was missing.

Cooper was missing. The noise, the mess, the conversation, the kisses, the cuddling on the sofa.

I'd spent three nights alone that week, so it wasn't like it was *that* different. But it was supposed to be our night, and I'd been looking forward to it.

I got into bed, trying not to think about how different my life had become in a matter of weeks or what that might have meant. I finally fell asleep, but the intercom buzzer woke me at one in the morning.

I staggered out to the living room and hit the intercom. "Lionel?"

"I'm very sorry to wake you, sir," he said. "But Mr. Jones is here."

"It's one in the morning," I mumbled. "Is everything okay? Is he hurt?"

"No, sir," Lionel replied. "He's drunk."

I sighed. "Can you send him up? Or should I come down and get him?"

"I'll get him into the elevator for you, sir."

"Thank you, Lionel."

Wearing only my sleep pants, I walked out to the elevator just as it arrived. The doors opened, and Cooper stood, leaning, half-falling against the back wall. I hit the door button so they stayed open, put my arm around him, and hauled him into my apartment.

"I'm sorry," he slurred. He planted his lips on mine. "You're so sexy."

I laughed. "You're drunk."

"'M sorry. Had to see you."

"It's okay, Cooper," I said, walking him down the hall to

my bedroom. "Everything okay? Did you have a good night?" Though it sure looked as though he had.

"'S good," he said. "Ryan knows I'm seein' someone." He fell onto the bed, and I stared at him, unable to speak. Then he mumbled, "Not you, o'course, just someone."

"Oh."

"He wanted to know who I've been spendin' my time with," he said, rolling onto his side. "But I didn't tell him."

My heart was beating double time, but I got into bed beside him. He was quiet for a little while and I assumed he was already asleep. But then he said, "Why won't you have sex with me?"

My heart leaped into my mouth. "What?"

His hand reached blindly for me, and now that my eyes had adjusted to the lack of light, I could see him watching me. "We've done everything else, why not that?" he asked, his voice slurred. "Don't you want me?"

I squeezed his hand. "Very much."

His voice was sleepy and not too coherent. "Then why?"

"Because it's something we can't come back from. If we do that," I clarified quietly, "what we have, what we're doing, becomes something else."

"Might want something else. More," he mumbled, and soon after, his breathing evened out and he started to snore.

I stared at the ceiling until morning, turning his words over and over in my head, while my heart tried to convince my brain that it might want something more too.

CHAPTER NINE

THE DOWNSIDE of being twenty-two was not knowing when you'd had enough to drink. The upside of being twenty-two was how quickly you recovered from drinking too much.

Whereas I'd have been hungover for an entire day, he woke up okay. He groaned a bit, didn't speak much, drank his coffee, then he drank mine. He swore he was never drinking again, told me it was my fault for letting him go out, showered, dressed in one of my older suits, and went to work.

He left before me, and as I walked through my lobby fifteen minutes later, Lionel winked at me. "He keeps you busy."

There was no point in denying it. "He does." Then I stopped walking. "Did he say anything to you last night?"

Lionel laughed. "Only that he couldn't understand why I didn't like him. I wasn't going to interrupt you, sir, but he wouldn't shut up," he said. "But this morning he was a little less talkative."

I couldn't help but chuckle. "Have a good day, Lionel."

"You too, sir."

I smiled all the way to work, and as I walked to my office, Jennifer being her usual professional self, smiled right back at me. "Good morning, Mr. Elkin. Coffee's on your desk."

It was a completely normal Friday. Busy, productive, but normal. I did see Cooper drink more coffee than normal, but he never missed a beat.

Then just before lunch, Jennifer knocked on my door. "Can I have a moment?"

I blinked in surprise but closed my laptop, giving her my undivided attention. "What is it?"

She sat down in a chair at my desk, something she'd never done before. "Your meeting with Mr. Takosama," she said quietly, "scheduled for next month in Tokyo, has been brought forward."

"Okay," I said, not fully understanding why she was being so cautious.

"He has two days free this week in Sydney, Australia. I took the liberty of securing the appointment," she said. "I know it's short notice, but it will give you less time to think of a reason not to go."

"Why wouldn't I want to go?"

Jennifer hesitated. "I booked two tickets."

"*Two* tickets?"

She swallowed and whispered, "I thought Mr. Jones could accompany you."

I stared at her. I had to tell myself to close my mouth while my brain caught up. There was no way Jennifer would say something like this, act so carefully if she wasn't sure.

Without any doubt in my mind, she knew.

"How did you know?" I asked quietly. "Did someone

say something? Has anyone in the office said anything?" Then a cold dread crept up my spine. "Did Cooper say something?"

"Oh, heavens no," she said. "He's not breathed a word of it. Going by him, I'd never have suspected a thing. But you, on the other hand..."

"Me?"

She smiled kindly at me. "It's the way you look at him."

"The way I what?"

"The way you look at him," she repeated. "Like the boy hung the moon." I went to correct her on the word 'boy' but she looked at me, daring me to argue. "I'm almost sixty. He's a boy to me. And there's the fact he's wearing the suit you bought last year."

I sighed and could feel myself blush. There was no point in denying it with her. So I confirmed what she already knew. "Yes, he's young, but he's smart, and he's so switched on. He has the tenacity and arrogance that comes with being twenty-something, but he's... I don't know... he's sweet and funny, and when we're together, there's no age difference between us." I didn't know why I was telling her this. But I needed to tell *someone*.

Jennifer smiled. "But?"

"But I don't know what I want. It took a lot for me to finally own up to my wife, and to myself, and admit that I was gay. It's been five years of finally living my real life, knowing exactly what I want, and knowing exactly who I am. But this is the first time that I don't know what I want at all."

Jennifer shook her head. "No, I think it's the first time you know *exactly* what you want." Then she sighed. "Tom." It was the first time she'd ever called me by my first name. "He makes you happy. I've never seen you so happy. It doesn't matter what anyone else thinks or says. It's about you."

There was a knock at the door. I didn't know whether to be sorry or grateful for the interruption. I cleared my throat. "Come in," I called out.

Of all people, it was Cooper. He stuck his head around the door, and when he saw Jennifer, without even saying hello, he said, "Oh, I can come back."

"No, it's fine," Jennifer said, standing up. "Mr. Jones, please come in."

Cooper did as he was bid but looked at the older lady nervously. She pursed her lips. "Have you got a passport?"

He looked at me, then back to Jennifer. "Yes?"

"Good," she said matter-of-factly. "You'll be going to Sydney with Mr. Elkin for four days. You leave tomorrow."

Cooper blinked. "Um..."

"Mr. Jones," Jennifer said brusquely. "Normally I would accompany Mr. Elkin on such trips, but my granddaughter is the first broccoli singing in a line of vegetables in her first-grade recital. I simply cannot miss it."

Cooper blinked again, and I think he tried not to smile. "Very well. I'm sure your granddaughter will be a great... broccoli..."

Jennifer stared at him. "You'll fly out tomorrow, six a.m. I've booked flights and accommodation, so if you need to make personal arrangements, please do so now," she said, shooing him, dismissing him.

The door closed behind him, and I looked at Jennifer and laughed. "You scare him, you know."

She smiled. "Oh, I know. Helps keep them in line."

I sighed. "And the trip to Sydney?"

"All legitimate, of course," she said with a sniff. "You *do* have a meeting with Mr. Takosama. He's expecting you. I have updated your schedule, and you'll be busy enough. But Mr. Jones will have a list a mile long of things to do." Then she softened. "But I thought you could use the time away."

I didn't know whether to laugh or cry. "Thank you, Jennifer."

"It's only four days," she said. "Being away from here will put a little perspective on things."

Four days. Four days in a different city. Four days to be ourselves.

"His internship is almost over," she said. "Four more weeks. You'll need to keep a lid on things until then."

"I know," I answered. "He knows that too."

She gave a curt nod. "What will you do after that?" she asked, looking me square in the eye. "Will you take him on here at the firm?"

I whispered, "I don't know."

"He's very good," she said from the door. "One of the best."

"Yes, he is."

"But?"

But I can't date a fellow employee. It's against company policy. Fuck, I was already so far in breach of company policy. Jennifer knew this. I presumed this was her point. "But... it's complicated."

"Yes, it is," she said. "For what it's worth, it's good to see you happy." She opened the door, then closed it quietly behind her.

I tried to get my head back into the job I was halfway through researching, but gave up and stared out across the blue skies of New York instead. Jennifer came in a few hours later, gave me files and instructions on the Takosama job, handed over the flight confirmation slips and accommodation reservation information, and told me to go home.

Figuring I had the next four days with Cooper, I suggested I pick him up from his place at half-past four in the morning. When he got in the car, despite the early hour, he was bright-eyed but quiet, obviously not wanting to speak in front of a company driver.

He was quiet as we checked in, and he was trying not to smile as we got coffee waiting to board. And by the time we finally got into our seats in first-class, he couldn't stop grinning. "This is awesome!" he whisper-shouted from the seat next to mine. "I can't believe Jennifer passed this up!"

"Jennifer knows about us," I told him as I got settled in. "She made you her replacement because she wanted us to have some time alone."

He was quiet, so I looked over at him. He was gaping. "She... she *knows*?"

I nodded. "Yes."

"How?"

I considered lying but decided to tell him the truth. "The way I look at you, apparently."

He stared at me and blinked, three, maybe four times, seemingly having lost the ability to speak. He fell back into his seat and looked pale.

I turned to face him and took his hand. "She won't tell a soul, I promise. She's the utmost professional, Cooper. She won't tell anyone."

"How can you be so sure?" he asked. "If she knows, then maybe someone else does?"

I shook my head. "No, she knows me, she knows me better than most people. She knew I'd separated from my wife by the fact I changed my cologne... well, that and the long hours and sleeplessness. But, believe me, no one else knows."

He sighed and seemed to relax. "By the way you look at me? What does that mean?"

"Apparently I smile when I see you," I told him seriously. "I'm trying to stop doing that."

"Right," he said with a laugh. "Look at me."

I did, I looked right at him. At his smirking lips, the slight dimple in his cheek, his bright and smiling eyes. And I smiled.

"Oh, you're hopeless," he said, shaking his head. Then he sighed dramatically. "Four days, huh? We've got four days before we have to go back to reality?"

I nodded. "We do have work to do on this trip."

"Oh, I know," he said. "The list Jennifer gave me is taller than the Empire State Building." He shook his head. "She gave it to me, I looked at it and she said if I couldn't manage it, she'd find someone more competent." Then he looked at me. "She doesn't like me, and now you tell me she knows we're... seeing each other?"

"She doesn't not like you," I told him. "She does it to keep you on your toes. In fact, she told me you were one of the best interns she'd ever seen."

"She said that?" he asked brightly. He sat back in his seat and smiled. "I *knew* she liked me."

I laughed at him. "Don't let on, though. She likes everyone to think she's mean."

He grinned like he had her all figured out, but as soon as we were at elevation, he pulled out his laptop and made a start on Jennifer's list.

WE ARRIVED at the Hilton in Sydney to find Jennifer had booked only one room.

"Is that a problem, sir?" the clerk asked.

Cooper answered quickly, "No, it's fine. We'll take it."

I glared at him, but he just grinned, signed us in, and took the key.

The room was extravagant and lovely, overlooking the city, and the view was spectacular. But the very large, *only* bed made me nervous. Sure, we'd slept in the same bed before, but this was different.

I knew what we were going to do in this bed.

I put my bags down, and despite how long we'd just spent on a plane, despite the time it was in Sydney, I looked at him nervously. "Wanna go and check out some sights?"

Cooper looked at the clock on the bedside table. "It's almost ten. What *sights* can we see at ten o'clock at night?"

"Let's go find out," I said.

"You know," Cooper said. He was staring at the huge, white bed. "This bed won't bite."

I looked at him quickly, then chuckled, embarrassed.

He laughed at me. "I might bite, but the bed won't."

I cleared my throat. "Come on, some air will do us good."

He rolled his eyes, sighed for effect, but then opened his suitcase and pulled out a jacket and beanie. "I can't believe we left summer to go somewhere it's winter. Who the hell does that?" he mumbled to himself.

I grabbed my coat too, and after I'd put it on, Cooper grabbed the key, then he grabbed my hand. "We can hold hands here," he said as we walked toward the elevator. "No one knows us."

I didn't object, and when I looked into the mirrored wall inside the elevator, Cooper smiled at us in the reflection. "Looking mighty fine tonight, Mr. Elkin," he said.

I looked at him in his winter coat and the beanie pulled over his hair. "Not too bad yourself, Mr. Jones."

He kissed my cheek quickly before the elevator doors opened, and he pulled me out through the lobby of the hotel and onto the street. He'd never been to Sydney before, and his excitement and enthusiasm were adorable.

The weather was cool, but we walked a few blocks, looking in shop windows, and there were even some souvenir shops and convenience stores still open. Cooper dragged me into some. He bought a few things as we went, some I looked at, some I waited outside for, and when he'd obviously seen enough, he declared he wanted to go back to the hotel.

We'd slept on and off on the plane, but figuring he must still be tired, I didn't mind. When we walked in, still holding hands, he led me straight to the bedroom. "Cooper, what are you doing?"

Then he upended one of the bags of things he'd just bought, and the contents spilled onto the bed.

A box of condoms and a bottle of lube.

I looked at Cooper, and before I could say anything, he took my face in his hands and kissed me. He held my face to his and kissed me like he'd never kissed me before. I could taste the urgency on his tongue, feel it in his hands.

He finally pulled his mouth from mine but still held my face to his. "Tom, I need you. Please."

I couldn't argue. I couldn't deny how much I wanted him. So I kissed him in a way that told him I would have him.

Not taking my mouth from his, I reached up and pulled his beanie off, then slipping my hands under his jacket, I pushed it off his shoulders.

He fumbled with my coat and tried too quickly to toe

out of his shoes. "Slow down, Cooper," I murmured against his lips. "It's okay, I'll take my time with you."

He nodded, and when he kissed me again, it was slower. He was calmer but no less certain.

I undressed him like I'd done plenty of times before, but this was different. I kissed down his neck. I ran my hands over every inch of skin I could reach. And he let me. He let me take charge. He wanted me to.

When he was naked, I told him to lie down on the bed and slowly undressed as I watched him. His long, taut body was stretched out before me, his erection lying heavy across his hip.

I started at his feet, running my hands up his legs, touching every part of him. I wanted his whole body to feel this, to react. When I got to his thighs, he spread them wide and pumped his cock with a groan.

I grabbed the lube and flipped the lid, smearing cool liquid over my fingers, then leaned up and kissed the head of his cock, running my tongue over the slit. He fisted my hair and moaned as I took all of him into my mouth, and while he was distracted with my tongue working over his dick, I rubbed his hole.

He cursed.

Then I swallowed around him and pressed one finger inside him. The sounds he made spurred me on. The more I worked him with my mouth, the more I stretched him, getting him ready for me. It wasn't long before he was begging me, so I turned my fingers, hooking them to the front until I found his gland.

He bucked his hips off the bed, fisted the sheets beside him, and threw his head back in a silent scream as he came.

Fuck, it was beautiful.

I pulled my fingers out, and he squirmed and writhed

through his orgasm, and I ripped open a foil wrapper and rolled on a condom. I pushed Cooper's legs up and open and pressed my cock against his ready ass.

I leaned over him and kissed his lips before slowly pushing inside him. His eyes widened, and he gasped, making me stop. "Are you okay?" I asked quickly.

"Yes." He nodded and gasped again. "More."

And with every inch I pressed into him, he gasped and pushed his head back into the pillow. I kissed along his strained neck, and he lifted his legs higher and held me tighter. "Fuck, Tom," he whispered. "Oh, fuck."

Only when I was buried inside him did I start to really move, rolling my hips into him. I held his face and kissed him. "I won't last long," I told him. "You feel too good."

Cooper slid his hand between us, taking his cock and pumping himself in time with my thrusts. "I need to come again."

Oh, fuck.

I leaned back to give him room, so I could watch him, so I could see where we were joined. Fuck. It was too much. "God, Cooper, come again for me."

He groaned and lifted his hips.

So I leaned over him again, thrusting harder, and I whispered into his ear, "I want to feel you come when I'm inside you."

And that did it.

He flexed against me, and he convulsed as his come splashed on my chest. But his ass clenched around me and I thrust hard one last time before I came. I was so lost in the sensation, so lost in the bliss, so lost in him.

When my senses came back to me, Cooper's arms were wrapped around me, his thighs still at my sides, and he was kissing my shoulder and my neck. "That was amazing," he whispered.

I chuckled into his neck, still too boneless to move. "You're amazing," I told him.

I could feel him smile into my neck. "While I really don't want to move, we need to shower."

I slowly pulled out of him, rolling us to our sides. But when he shivered from the cold, I took him into the shower.

I poured shampoo into my hand and lathered it into his hair to wash the lube out.

"What time is the meeting tomorrow?" he asked.

"Ten a.m.," I answered. "Lean your head back," I told him and washed the soap from his hair. "There you go."

"Is it all out?"

"Yep, you have lube-free hair."

He laughed, and when we were out of the shower and dried off, he climbed back into bed, naked. He patted the bed beside him, so, as naked as him, I joined him and we fell asleep wrapped in each other's arms.

I woke up spooning Cooper. Actually, I woke up to Cooper wiggling his ass against my hardening cock.

When he knew I was awake, he took my hand and rolled onto his stomach, pulling me on top of him, over him.

"Are you sore?" I asked gruffly into the back of his neck.

He shook his head. "Mm-mm, no." Then he spread his legs and raised his ass. "Want you."

"Jesus," I said with a groan. "Are you sure?"

"Please."

Fuck. Reaching over, I grabbed the supplies off the bedside table. I sheathed myself first, then slicked him with lube. He writhed as I prepped him and lifted his ass higher. "Tom, please, baby, please."

I pressed against him, inside him, and sank all the way

in in one long push. He groaned like I'd never heard him before. He was vocal, not a quiet lover, not a shy lover. If he wanted it, he asked for it, or he just took it.

I kissed the back of his neck as I thrust into his ass, and he slid his hand underneath himself. I leaned up on my knees and pulled his ass up so I could fill him and so he could pleasure himself.

It wasn't long before he came with a sharp cry, making me follow soon after.

We collapsed onto the sticky bed, sated and chuckling. "Good morning," he said with a laugh.

I kissed his shoulder. "Good morning."

"Maybe we shouldn't sleep naked," he said.

"Or maybe we should."

He squeezed his dick and groaned. "Jesus, I could almost go again."

I rolled off him. "God, you'll be the death of me."

He laughed, rolled off the bed, and slapped my ass. "Up with you, Mr. Elkin. We have a great deal to get done today."

* * *

THE MEETING with Takosama was long. But considering the sizeable account and the fact we'd just spent twenty-one hours flying to meet with him, it was imperative we were productive.

I'd met with him before. We'd worked on his last build together. He wanted the best for his Fourth Avenue address, and he'd gotten the best when he asked for me. This was a different project, his second home, but no less important to him.

He ran businesses in Japan, Australia, and America,

and he had two days free while in Sydney, so that was where I fitted in. We discussed plans and conceptual designs all day. Then I'd go back and draft them up that night and show them to him the next day. He'd either approve them or hire someone else.

I spent the day with him in his George Street office, while Cooper sat in the corner quietly taking notes. It was how Takosama did business. He dealt with one man, the man in charge, and only him.

It wasn't strictly how I preferred to do business, but Cooper didn't seem to mind. He said he understood the cultural differences and seemed happy to be in the background writing madly as we talked. He didn't eat with us, and when Takosama was called out for an important phone call, I asked Cooper if he was okay.

"Sure," he said with a smile, then went back to writing.

When the meeting was over, Cooper quietly packed away his notepad and pen and stood quietly waiting. When Mr. Takosama addressed him, Cooper bowed his head politely, then he did something no one was expecting.

He spoke in Japanese.

I was floored, and Takosama was very pleased. He gave me an honest smile, shook my hand again, and we left. As we climbed into a cab to go back to the hotel, I still couldn't believe it. "What the hell did you say to him?"

"Nothing much," he said with a smile. "I simply told him it was an honor to sit in with him."

"Why the hell didn't you tell me you knew Japanese?"

"I don't really," he said. "I studied cultural etiquette at college."

I shook my head. "You're a surprise at every turn."

He grinned at that, then he pulled out his notepad. "I have a lot of notes."

"I have a pretty good idea of what he's after."

Cooper nodded. "I know. You were incredible in there today."

That night, for the next few hours, I drew up some concepts for the job while Cooper worked on the specifications. I had to admit, we worked well as a team. But by the time we were done and jet lag had well and truly kicked in, we fell into bed and slept.

The meeting with Takosama the next day took ten minutes. He looked over the plans, studying each one carefully, read through the spec sheets Cooper had done, and he smiled. He shook my hand, then Cooper's, and by ten fifteen that morning, we'd won the contract.

Which gave us two full days off.

Cooper was still buzzed about the Takosama job and his excitement was palpable. We got in some sightseeing, though he was more interested in the buildings than in things like the Harbour Bridge or Bondi Beach.

He marveled at the Sydney Opera House. He sat on the steps and just shook his head in wonder. Dragging him from the modern icon, I took him into the oldest part of Sydney, where the buildings were made of sandstone.

Watching him, as he took in the history and the designs of each building I showed him, was priceless. He commented on the British colonial influences, which led to a discussion on England, and he said he'd never been.

"Oh, London is beautiful," I told him. "I'll take you one day and show you some of the most incredible places. And Paris and Prague. The history in those cities is mind-blowing."

His whole face lit up. "Really? You'd take me and show me?"

I would. I was starting to think I'd take him anywhere,

show him anything to see him smile like that. I nodded. "Yes."

He just beamed, and for the rest of the afternoon, he seemed content to just be with me, enjoying the quiet peacefulness between us. But then as it got later and as I was thinking of bed, he shook his head.

"Enough old fuddy-duddy stuff for one day," he said. "Now it's my turn."

"Your turn for what?"

He grinned. "Get dressed, old man. We're going out."

CHAPTER TEN

"A NIGHTCLUB?" I repeated. "Really?"

"Yes, really," he answered, pulling on a tight-fitting tee. I was going to argue the point, but then he said, "We can't go out together back home. I can't dance with you. I can't be seen with you because of work. But we can here."

I couldn't argue with that.

As we got in the cab and Cooper gave directions, I asked him how he knew where to go. "I asked the doorman," he said, as though it should have been obvious. Then he added, "The one who checked you out every time you walked past."

"Checked me out?"

Cooper laughed at me. "You should get your eyes tested."

"My eyes are just fine," I said indignantly.

He took my hand and gave it a squeeze. "Half the men we walk past look at you, and you have no idea."

We pulled up at wherever Cooper had given directions to and got out onto the busy sidewalk. It was late and cold, but there were people walking to and from venues up and down the street. Cooper pulled my hand and led me straight into one club, and the first thing I noticed was that they were mostly all men.

We showed our IDs, the security guy took a second look at mine, but we walked in and headed toward the bar. Cooper pulled me in close, and I griped in his ear, "The guy at the door had to look twice at my ID."

He leaned in close so I could hear him over the music. "Because you look so good for your age."

I rolled my eyes and looked around the crowded room. I was easily the oldest man there by about ten years. "They probably think you're here with your father."

Cooper grabbed my face and kissed me right there in a crowded bar, for anyone to see. "Now they don't think I'm here with my father," he said. He leaned over the bar, ordered two drinks, and looked at me. "Now drop the age thing. We're here to dance, okay?"

And that was what we did. We danced.

He led the way, of course. I'd expected nothing less. But he wasted no time in putting his hands on me, pulling me in close, and making us sway. He kissed my neck and my lips, but it was easy to tell he was lost in the music.

The room was too crowded and the music was too loud, but his eyes were closed, his lips were curled in a small smile as he moved, and I didn't care about anything else. He was beautiful to watch.

I ran my hands over his back, over his ass, and as I ran my hands up his sides, he lifted his arms above his head and swayed. He never opened his eyes; he never stopped smiling. But he danced, and I pulled him tighter against me, and his arms came down around me.

I didn't know how long we danced for. I didn't fucking care. If he wanted to dance—if that was what twenty-two-year-olds wanted to do—then I'd gladly do it with him.

We got back to the hotel at some ungodly hour. He pulled me onto the bed, and instead of having sex, I sixty-nined him.

We woke up late, spent a lazy day shopping and taking in the foreign city. He was right. It was nice to be able to just be with him. We were free to just walk around, to be ourselves, without fear of being spotted by someone we worked with. And in New York we couldn't do that. Granted, it was a much bigger city, but there were eyes watching everywhere there, and someone would be bound to see us together and question why.

By mid-afternoon we were back in bed, both of us sated and breathing heavily. He was threading his fingers through the hair on my chest.

"Maybe we should get some sleep," I suggested. "We need to check out of here at four in the morning."

Cooper shook his head and pulled himself on top of me, sucking my nipple into his mouth. "No, you can sleep on the plane. I'm not done with you yet."

WALKING BACK through the airport terminal in New York for me was bittersweet. I loved coming home, but I also didn't want my time in Sydney to end. Cooper sighed. "Wish we had four more days."

"Me too," I replied honestly.

"What happens from here?" he asked quietly. It was rare to see him so unsure.

"What do you mean?"

He shrugged. "Well, my internship is up in four weeks..."

I wasn't sure what he was alluding to. Whether it was that he'd no longer be an employee or whether he assumed I'd make him a full-time employee, I wasn't sure. "Things will be different, yes."

He nodded slowly. "Good different or bad different?"

"That depends on a lot of things that aren't necessarily within my control," I answered, knowing he'd understand I was referring to work. "But I'm hoping for the former of the two."

He smiled. "That's good to know."

"Cooper, please understand, I'm not the one who decides if interns stay or go," I told him. "Sometimes none of them do. Sometimes all the interns get is the experience they can take with them."

"I know that," he said. "I wasn't implying that you... I didn't mean for you to..." I'd never seen him struggle for words before. "I know that," he said again. But then he smiled. "Just means we have to make the most of the next four weeks."

We met the driver, he threw our luggage in the trunk of the car, and we dropped Cooper home first. It was back to Mr. Elkin and Mr. Jones in the car and at work the next morning.

Jennifer came in with my morning coffee and asked me how the trip went. I told her we'd secured the Takosama job, to which she replied she already knew. "Did Mr. Jones get through his to-do list?" she asked.

I smiled at her. "Yes, he was very... good."

She smiled at my choice of words. "Good to hear. Any chance to think on that perspective we discussed before you left?"

"Yes."

"And?"

"I'm happy with what I've got," I answered. "Just not sure on how to keep it."

"I'm sure you'll think of a way."

I sighed. "Well, I hope so." Then I thought of something. "Is Cooper in yet? I haven't seen him."

"Yes," Jennifer answered. "Though I think he's avoiding me. I presume you told him I know about you two?"

I smiled at her. "Yes, I told him. And yes, now he's twice as scared of you." But I stood up and walked with her out of my office. "The Takosama file. Where is it?"

"With Donella."

"And Cooper's at his desk?"

"He was, yes."

I walked down the hall to the cubicle area where the interns and other office staff were. I spotted him talking to the other interns, and before I got to him, one of the draftsmen stopped me to discuss something.

That was when I heard what Cooper was saying. They were discussing Sydney. "Yeah, it's really beautiful, but the weather was cooler than I expected. I'd like to go back in summer," he said.

"How was the big meeting?" one girl asked.

"Oh, it was so good," he told them. "Sitting in there with them while they talked business. It was kind of surreal."

"And what was Mr. Elkin like?" someone else asked. "Did you see much of him?"

My heart stopped in my chest, waiting for his answer. I finished talking to the draftsman and walked slowly over toward Cooper.

"Nah, he spent his time doing whatever, and I did my thing," he answered. But then he looked up at me walking toward him, then back to his little audience, and smiled when he said, "He's old anyway. What is he? Like fifty-five?"

"Good morning," I said loudly, and every intern there, besides Cooper, looked up at me and scattered in every direction, suddenly very, very busy.

It was almost comical. Cooper certainly tried not to smile. The little shit.

"Mr. Jones? A moment please."

"Certainly, Mr. Elkin," he said, standing up. How he kept a straight face, I'll never know.

I told him with my eyes he was in trouble, to which he replied with his eyes that he'd enjoy every moment of it.

"The Takosama file is with Donella. She's one of my head drafters. I thought you might like to follow the job through its stages, considering you were there at inception."

His eyes lit up. "I'd love to."

Then with a stern voice for the benefit of the intern audience, I added, "Though I can probably think of *fifty-five* reasons to have you archive files for the rest of your stay here."

Cooper bit the inside of his lip to stop from smiling, but the poor girl next to him who was staring at her computer screen trying not to listen to us made an odd whining sound. Cooper smiled. "That won't be necessary, sir," he said.

"I'll let Donella know to expect you," I told him. "But you can report to my office before you leave today."

Sure enough, at a quarter to six, Jennifer's line buzzed. "Mr. Jones to see you."

"Thank you."

He walked in and sat in the seat across from me, but he didn't speak.

I raised my eyebrows at him. "Fifty-five?"

Then he burst out laughing. "Oh, my God," he said as he laughed. "That was the funniest thing I've seen."

"The poor girl next to you was almost beside herself."

He laughed again. "She thought you were gonna send me packing."

"I should have," I told him. "I should have kicked your ass out." Maybe he would have taken me seriously if I weren't smiling when I said it. I shook my head at him and finally laughed. "You're such a little shit."

He cracked up laughing at that, but then Jennifer walked in and Cooper sat up in his seat and straightened out his suit as he tried to stop smiling, which of course made me laugh.

"Not so funny now, is it?"

He shook his head at me, then glanced nervously at Jennifer. She looked at me, obviously not used to seeing me laugh. "I'll be heading home soon, Mr. Elkin. Are you working late or from home tonight?"

"Yes," I told her. "Home tonight. I'll be leaving soon, but I have some work to catch up on."

"You missed lunch today, so I can order something for you to eat before I leave, if you'd like," she said.

The sound of food sounded good. "Actually, that'd be great," I told her. "Thai fish, delivered to home around eight would be lovely, thank you."

Jennifer gave me a smile, then turned to Cooper. "Mr. Jones?"

Cooper's eyes darted to mine, then back to Jennifer. "Pardon?"

I smiled at Jennifer. "He'll have the same as me, and he likes those Thai vegetable rolls."

"Very well," she said and walked out of the door.

Cooper stared at me, wide-eyed and open-mouthed. "What just happened?"

"Jennifer just included you in my dinner order."

His eyes lit up. "Oh, that sounds like fun."

"I didn't mean I was having you for dinner."

"But you can."

I sighed and closed my laptop. "See you at my place in half an hour?"

"Sure," he answered. Then as he walked to the door, he said, "Tell Lionel I'll see him then."

FOR THE NEXT THREE WEEKS, we worked together, professionally and discreetly, and spent time together in the privacy of our apartments.

I had no qualms about going to his place because, to put it plainly, no one who knew me professionally would ever be anywhere near Cooper's small, not-luxury apartment on East sixty-first street. And if anyone spotted Cooper entering my building, they'd presume he was running errands for me. My interns worked when I did, and I worked all the time.

At the end of the third week, we'd spent an incredible Friday night finishing off some prelims at my dining table, then finishing each other off on the sofa, before moving to the bedroom where we'd spent the night trying to break our record for how many times we could have sex in one night.

He had the libido of a twenty-two-year-old guy, and I told him I'd die trying to keep up with him. He laughed and told me, "At least you'll die happy," right before he took my cock in his mouth.

Fucking hell.

I knew the countdown to the end of his internship was approaching, but he never brought it up again. Neither did I.

We just spent our time talking and laughing. And fucking. He was insatiable.

By the time we got out of bed on Saturday, it was almost lunchtime. I woke up to hear him in the shower, which was a little odd, but he came out wearing just a towel and a grin. He straddled me, shoving his semi-hard dick near my mouth and told me he'd showered so I could rim him.

No doubt about it. If he wanted something, he just asked. Or, in more cases than not, he *told* me.

I didn't mind. Hell, I didn't mind at all.

So I threw him off me, pinned him face first on my bed, and gave him just what he asked for. I left him a quivering, sated lump on the bed and started the shower. He joined me a short while later, but I told him no more sex until we'd both eaten at least.

I left him in the bathroom, pulled on a pair of cargos, and went in search of food. I had half the contents of the fridge on the bench, a couple of plates, had the coffee brewing, my stomach was growling, and life was pretty fucking good.

Then there was a knock on the door.

There were only a very few select people who Lionel wouldn't buzz through, and I didn't have to wonder for long when Ryan's voice called out. "Dad?"

Shit.

Shit, shit, shit.

"Um," I answered. "Coming," I said, and when I unlocked the door, Ryan looked at my very rarely worn casual cargos, my shirtless torso, and my still-wet hair.

"Did I get you out of the shower?"

"Uh, yeah..." I hesitated, walking back to the kitchen. "I was just making something to eat."

"No worries," he said brightly. "Just haven't seen you much lately, thought I'd stop by." Then there was the sound of a door closing. Ryan turned his head toward the hall, then glanced back at me. "Is someone else here?" he asked. Then he grinned. "Do you have *company?*"

"Um, kind of..."

Fuck.

Then Cooper walked out, wearing only his underwear, holding up the new toothbrush I'd bought for him. "Tom, did you get me..."

And his words died away, as did his smile.

There were excuses I could give why Cooper was coming to and from my apartment lobby with his messenger bag, but there was no reason whatsoever I could give to explain why he had walked out of my bedroom in his under-wear. Except the truth.

The three of us stared at each other, mouths open and silent, then both of them looked at me.

"Ryan," I started, but he held up his hand. He took a step back from me, then he turned and bolted for the door.

CHAPTER ELEVEN

COOPER WAS QUICK. I didn't think I'd ever seen him run. Certainly not in his underwear, holding a toothbrush, but he beat Ryan to the door.

"What the fuck, man?" Ryan cried.

"You're not leaving until you hear us out," Cooper told him.

Ryan stared at him but pointed to me. "That's my dad, man!"

"I know that," Cooper said calmly, still holding the toothbrush like it wielded some magical power. "Please. Just sit and listen."

Ryan shook his head, but he turned to me, where I stood half-dressed and helpless near the kitchen counter. The fight in him was gone, or the flight, as the case might be, and Cooper walked him to the sofa and sat him down.

Ryan was now pale and looking a little sick. I took a seat beside him and sighed. "It's a long story," I said rather pathetically.

"Oh, Jesus," he breathed. "You're not even denying it!"

Then he started to breathe erratically, like he was going to hyperventilate or throw up. Cooper disappeared into the kitchen and came back with a paper bag. I didn't even know I had paper bags. "Here, breathe into that," he instructed. "Put your head between your knees."

"I'm not on a fucking plane," Ryan said, but snatched the bag and started to breathe into it.

Cooper kneeled down in front of him, still wearing just his briefs and still holding the toothbrush. "Ry, Tom and I have been seeing each other for about six weeks."

Ryan lowered the paper bag. "The guy you've been seeing, the one you were all so secret-squirrel about, *was my dad?*"

Cooper nodded. "Yes."

"Oh, fucking hell," Ryan squeaked. "The one you said sucked dick like a Dyson?"

Cooper shrugged and shot me a not-even-sorry glance. "I was drunk..."

I fell back on the sofa and groaned, and Ryan put the paper bag back to his mouth and started to breathe into it again.

"Look," Cooper said. "Ryan, it's complicated."

Ryan nodded and spoke into the bag. "Tell me about it." Then his eyes fell to what Cooper was holding. "You have a toothbrush here?"

"Tom just bought it for me," he answered with a smile.

Ryan huffed into the paper bag. "You call him Tom?" Then Ryan gaped at me. "He calls you Tom?"

I nodded. "Ryan, we never meant to keep anything from you. I never meant to have secrets or to go behind your back, but this thing between Cooper and me is... Well, it's complicated."

He lowered the bag. "So you keep saying."

"No one can know," Cooper said. "We work together, I'm an intern at your father's firm, and they have these policies..."

Ryan turned slowly to stare at me. "You'd risk your precious fucking career for him?"

"Ryan," I warned, but it was Cooper who spoke.

"It's mine, Ryan. It's my career he's protecting," he said quietly. "If we were found out, Tom would get no more than a slap on the wrist, but me? I'd be lucky to get a job cleaning floors."

Ryan shook his head. "So why the hell do it?"

"Why do you think?" Cooper asked. "Jesus, Ryan."

"You *like* him?" Ryan asked, staring at Cooper. "You're serious about him?"

Cooper looked at me, then at the floor. He nodded and whispered, "Yes."

I smiled, despite the whole unfolding scene. Ryan turned to me, he saw me smile at Cooper, and he rolled his eyes. "And you like him? You want to be with him?"

I was still smiling at Cooper when I answered. "Yes."

"How very fucking Disney," Ryan cried, putting the paper bag back to his mouth. He breathed into it a few times, then lowered it. "He's the same age as me!"

"I know that," I answered quietly. Ryan was angry, and I guessed well within his rights to be so.

Then he stared at Cooper. "My dad?" he asked. "Dude! If older guys are your thing, then find someone else who's not my father!"

Cooper gave him a sad smile. He scratched his head and sighed. "Ry, do you remember back when we were in the twelfth grade and you had it so bad for that Rebecca chick?

And she was such a bitch, and we all hated her, but you wanted her?" Cooper asked, and Ryan stared at him, confused.

It was weird for me to hear Cooper talk like the twenty-two-year-old he was, and I wondered what he was talking about too, but then he explained. "Well, this is a bit like that," he said, nodding to himself. "We were playing with you, but when you told me you were serious, I let it go. Regardless of what I thought, I did everything I could to help to help you date her, and you told me it meant a lot, remember that?"

Ryan nodded.

Then he was back to the Cooper I knew. "So, Ryan, you need to let it go," Cooper said simply and seriously. "You need to grow up and realize this isn't about you. I'm sorry to put it like that, but that's just the way it is. What we do, or what goes on between me and your father, ultimately doesn't concern you."

Ryan stared at him. "If you're gonna lecture me, can you at least put on some freakin' clothes?" Then Ryan looked at me. "I fucking hate it when he gets all 'I'm tellin' ya how it is' like that. He was like it when we were in high school. He's still fucking like it. He should have been a cop, or a teacher, or a lawyer."

I smiled. "He's fairly straightforward, yes."

Cooper smiled, and the air between the three of us seemed to relax. He stood up and groaned loudly. "You'd think I'd be used to being on my knees by now."

Ryan put the bag back to his face and breathed into it with a groan. "Coop, don't."

Cooper walked toward the hall. "I'm gay. There will always be dick jokes."

Ryan looked at me like it was my fault. I held my hands up. "No dick jokes from me."

"I should think not," Ryan said. Then he leaned back on the sofa, let his hand holding the paper bag fall to his thigh, and sighed. He took a few deep breaths. "Does Mom know?"

"No, of course not," I told him. "No one knows. Well, Jennifer knows, and now you do."

"And you really like him?"

I nodded. "I never expected it, and I never went looking. We started working together and it just kind of evolved." I looked around to make sure Cooper was still out of the room. "We're not even sure if it's going anywhere. We really don't know if it *can* go any further. It just is what it is at the moment. It was never supposed to get serious, with work and all..."

"You weren't kidding when you said it was complicated."

I snorted. "No. And Cooper's right. We need this to stay quiet."

Ryan nodded. "Who the fuck would I tell?" he asked rhetorically. "They'd all think I was bullshitting them anyway."

"How about I finish making that coffee?"

Ryan nodded. "Good idea." Then he added, "How about you put a shirt on while you're at it?"

"Deal," I said, and as I walked to the hall, Cooper walked out. I whispered, "Be nice."

I got to the door of my room when I heard Cooper say, "Hey, douchenozzle, help me get lunch ready."

I took a deep breath and walked into my robe to get a shirt.

RYAN LEFT LATER THAT AFTERNOON, and I thought he was okay with it. We'd had lunch, and Cooper and he had been acting like old times before he'd left, so I presumed he was okay.

He'd said he was okay with it. He'd said he wouldn't tell anyone, but he'd said he'd need some time and asked us to refrain from displays of affection in front of him so he didn't completely freak the fuck out.

His words, not mine. But I agreed wholeheartedly. I had really only gotten my relationship with Ryan back after the split with his mother, so all things considered, he'd taken the news pretty well.

But things between Cooper and I were different after that. Someone outside of us, outside of Jennifer, knew about us. It made it more... real.

We'd admitted, while not to each other, but to Ryan, that we liked each other and that we were serious about this. And that made it more real.

And of course it was the last week of Cooper's internship, which also made it more real. We were on a deadline, of sorts. One way or another, something would change, and now that we'd admitted feelings, it made something already complicated even more complicated.

It was never supposed to be complicated. It was never supposed to be anything. I certainly was never supposed to be involved with a man I worked with, a man half my age. I was never supposed to have feelings for him or to enjoy every moment I spent with him.

And as the days drew closer, as the final week wound down, it was the whopping big elephant in the room I was never supposed to deal with.

Cooper seemed to pretend it wasn't an issue, so I did too, despite how much it worried me. The bottom line was, if I told the board I wanted him to stay at Brackett and Golding, then we couldn't be together. If I told them I didn't want him to work at the firm, then he'd never forgive me. Sure, it wasn't my pending decision, but my opinion held water in the firm. If I told them he was as good as I thought he was, they'd want to keep him for sure. It wasn't fair to him because he was good, and he deserved to work at the best architectural firm in New York.

And like a light bulb popping up over my head, I picked up my phone. "Jennifer, can you get Louisa Arlington's number?"

THE MEETING on Friday afternoon to decide the fate of the interns was awful. I sat there with my head turned, looking out of the window, unable to bear looking at Cooper.

When his name wasn't called as one of the interns offered employment, he stood for a moment, then professionally thanked the other partners for their time and experience before he walked out.

I didn't watch him leave. I couldn't. I felt nauseated, and after I'd sat in my office wondering what the fuck I'd just done, I told Jennifer I wasn't feeling well and I left.

She was concerned about me, probably just as confused by my actions as Cooper. She knew I liked him. She saw how happy he made me, and she'd just seen me throw it away.

I couldn't bear to look at her either.

I went home and threw myself onto the sofa and buried

my face in my hands. Not long after, the intercom buzzed and Lionel's voice said, "I tried to stop him, but Mr. Jones is on his way up. Should I call the police?"

I got up and pressed the button. "No, it's fine."

"He's quite upset, sir."

I nodded, though Lionel couldn't see. "I know."

Then there was banging on the door. "Tom, open the door. I know you're in there."

I walked slowly to the door, unlocked it and let it swing open. Cooper walked inside and started yelling. "So is that it? What was I, just some summer fuck? Was that all I ever was?"

"Absolutely not," I said quickly.

"Was any of what you said to Ryan the other day true?" he asked. He was clearly upset and very angry. "You told him you liked me. Was that a fucking lie too?"

"No."

"Then why did you tell them not to hire me?"

"I told you it wasn't my final decision, Cooper."

"That's bullshit and you know it. Whatever the almighty Thomas Elkin wants, he gets."

I shook my head. "That's not true."

"Bull. Shit," he said through clenched teeth.

"So was the only reason you were so interested in me was because you thought I could get you a job?"

"What?" he cried. "No, fucking hell, Tom, no! Every single fucking thing I've said to you is the truth. I didn't expect you to get me a job because of *us*. If any interns got offered a job, I would have expected a shot because I'm fucking good at what I do. They hired Anna, and I'm better than her."

"You are!" I said. "You're the best!"

"So put me on the ground floor," he said. "I'll work my way up. I'll be someone's fucking assistant, I don't care."

"You're too good to be an assistant. You've got too much talent to be in anyone's shadow, particularly mine. You need to prove that you can do it on your own and not because of who you're with."

"You're not hiring me because I'm too talented?" He threw his hands up. "Jesus Christ! What kind of fucked-up logic is that?"

"The logic that keeps us together!" I yelled back at him. "If you stay at Brackett and Golding, we can't be together. Not permanently, not ever. We could hide it for two or three months when you were working with me as an intern, but on a permanent basis... it just wouldn't work." Then I stared at him. "I don't want to hide anymore. I want more than that."

He shook his head, not believing a word I was saying.

So I told him, "I've lined up an interview at Arlington Initiative for you. They have the same reputation as us. I've specifically called in this favor, telling Louisa Arlington you're the best I've seen. I told her you have ten times the talent I had at your age, and I sent over some of your work. She wants to meet you. Tuesday morning, ten o'clock. I've worked with her. She'll give you more than what I could."

"You *what?*"

I nodded. "You should work for the best."

"I want to work for you!"

"You'll go further with someone else!"

Cooper shook his head. "*Why?* Cut the crap and tell me the real reason *why?*"

"Because I want you to move in with me," I told him. "I want you to live with me, to be with me. I want to be with you and we can't do that if we work together."

He stared at me with his mouth open.

"If you work at Brackett and Golding, you won't be taken seriously. Your work will be discredited because of me, because if we're together they'll assume you only got the job, got promoted, got whatever, *because of me*. Can't you see that?"

He shook his head. "And who the fuck lets you decide?" he yelled at me. "What makes you think I wouldn't choose the job over you?"

I stared at him. "What?"

"You're so sure we were going to be together, you're so fucking certain that we'll be together so you decide I can't work there," he spat out. "What if I wanted the job and not you? If we're not together, then I can work there, yes?"

I couldn't speak. My heart was hammering. Breaking. I nodded, and my voice croaked. "I guess."

He walked up to me. His jaw was clenched and he pointed his finger into my chest. "You don't make that decision for me." He backed off, then paced around my apartment, picking up his things and putting them in his bag. "And you don't ask me to move in with you like that. You don't ask someone to be with you in the middle of an argument, Tom." He shoved a shirt into his bag.

I looked at him packing his things. "What are you doing?"

"I'm going to my apartment," he said. "I need some time without you telling me what to do, without you telling me how to live my fucking life."

"I didn't mean to," I said weakly. "That's not what I meant. I had about two minutes to make a decision. I didn't have time to find you, to speak to you, so I called Louisa. I thought I was doing the right thing, for you, for us..."

"Without asking me," he said simply. "Without any consideration for what *I* want."

"Cooper, please."

But without another word, he picked up his bag, turned, and walked out of the door.

After the yelling, after all the things he'd said, the silence he left behind was the hardest thing to deal with.

CHAPTER TWELVE

THE NEXT FOUR days were hell.

I didn't sleep. I couldn't eat. On Saturday and Sunday, I worked at home, even though everything reminded me of him. He still had clothes and a pair of shoes at my place, and I hoped he'd call me asking if he could come and get them. He never did.

I left a message on the second day, saying I was sorry for being an overbearing ass. He didn't call me back. I went to his apartment. He wasn't home. Or he pretended he wasn't.

I was fucking pathetic.

Ryan came by on Sunday night. He walked in, took one look at me, and shook his head. "Jesus. And I thought Cooper looked like shit."

I sat up straighter. "Have you seen him? Is he okay?"

"He's fine," Ryan answered, and his words stung.

"Oh," I said quietly. Then I realized that was a good thing for Cooper. "Well, good, I guess. I'm glad he's okay." I hardly sounded convincing. "Did he say anything about me?" I asked and regretted it almost immediately.

"Don't even think about it," Ryan said flatly. He leaned

against the kitchen counter and crossed his arms. "Don't think about putting me in the middle of this, because I won't even go there. Don't make me pick sides. You both got yourselves into this mess."

I sighed and scrubbed my hand over my face. "Fair enough." Then I admitted, "It was my mess. I fucked up."

Ryan didn't even bat an eyelid at my cuss. "I know. He told me."

"Is he still mad at me?"

Ryan snorted. "You've met him, right? He's a stubborn, self-righteous ass. Of course he's still mad."

I nodded. "I shouldn't have done what I did."

"Yes, you should have," Ryan said. His tone was softer. "But maybe you just should have told him about it first."

"I know," I said, sighing again. "He asked for some time."

"Then give him that."

I nodded but said nothing.

"Jesus, you really do have it bad, don't you?"

I looked at my son. "I wasn't expecting this," I said as a poor way of answering. "I wasn't expecting... him."

Ryan exhaled loudly, walked over to my sofa, and threw himself onto it. "So, pizza for dinner?"

I smiled at the welcome distraction. "Sounds good."

Ryan didn't mention Cooper again, but we watched some TV and talked a bit, and it was nice. It was nice of him, knowing I had no one else I could talk about this to, because no one else knew Cooper and I were ever together.

Not that we'd really ever been *together*, either. We'd never discussed anything; we'd never put a label on what we had. We'd just been... us.

That realization, that we'd never officially been

anything, made me realize just how foolish I'd been. I'd never told him outright how I felt.

On Monday, after I left another pathetic, barely whispered apology on his voicemail, I spent the entire day staring out across the city, waiting for him to call.

He never did.

By Tuesday, I had myself convinced that whatever we'd had was finished and that I was an asshole and I deserved his silence. His absence. I knew what I'd done was wrong, how it had ended was wrong, and I needed to pull my shit together. I arrived at work determined to be productive, and it was going well. Burying myself in work to avoid my life had worked for twenty years, so it really shouldn't have been so difficult. I opened files, opened my laptop, and for a few hours, I managed to not stare into space.

Just before lunch, Jennifer knocked on my door, opened it without my saying so, and stood aside. Cooper walked in, dressed in his business suit, looking very professional. His chin was raised; his eyes were determined.

I put my pen down and had to close my mouth. I'd missed him so much. Just seeing him made my heart clench. I was filled with equal parts hope that he was here to say he forgave me and dread that he would say we were over.

I was expecting to hear goodbye. And when Jennifer closed the door and Cooper sat down across from me, after wanting to see him and speak to him for four fucking days, now I wasn't sure I wanted him to say anything. Hearing him say it was over would make it so final.

"I'm really sorry," I said quickly.

He put his hand up, clearly still angry with me. "Will you let me speak?"

I nodded. "Of course."

"I just came out from my meeting with Louisa Arlington."

"Oh?"

"I suppose I should thank you."

"You're welcome," I told him, though I wasn't sure if he was happy about it. "And I'm very sorry."

He ignored my apology. "She spoke very highly of you."

"Louisa's lovely and very good at her job," I said quietly. "She's one of the best there is."

"She said the same of you." Then he smiled. "Actually, she said you were the *second*-best there was. She was the first."

"Sounds like her," I said softly. He was still angry, and I didn't blame him. "Cooper, I'm really sorry. I fucked up, and I'm sorry."

"You did," he said flatly. But then he sighed. "You were also right."

"Huh?"

"You were right," he said with the start of a smile. "I couldn't work with you or for you. It would have hindered my career. You were right about that. I can see that now."

I wasn't sure if he was agreeing with me or insulting me, but either way, I nodded. "I'm still sorry." He had no idea how much. I didn't know what else to say, and he looked like he was done talking. My voice was quiet. "How did it go with Louisa?"

"I start on Monday."

My eyes widened. "That's really good, Cooper. She really is one of the best."

"Hmm," he hummed. Then he looked around my office. "She also said something interesting."

"What was that?"

"She also said you told her why you wanted me to work

with her," he said. "She said she was confused at first. Because if I was as good as you said I was, she didn't understand why you didn't want me to work here with you."

I nodded. "I told her the truth."

"Did you?"

I looked at him, fairly certain I knew what he was talking about. I nodded again. "I told her you'd be better off, professionally, with her."

"Well, she agreed with you on that." He looked me square in the eye. "Then she told me what you really said. She said she knew I had to be something special for you to call her and ask her for a favor, so she asked you what was so remarkable about me."

I nodded. Yep, he knew.

Cooper shook his head. "She said you told her I *was* special, that I couldn't work here with you no matter how much you wanted me to because you have feelings for me and you'd rather I *live* with you than *work* with you." Then he spoke slowly, enunciating every syllable. "Because you have feelings for me."

I looked at him, and I knew he saw the truth, the fear in my eyes. I didn't answer. I didn't have to.

He glared at me. "You inconsiderate bastard," he said, and my eyes shot to his. "Do you know what it's like to hear that from someone else?"

I shook my head. "I shouldn't have said that to her. I'm sorry."

"Damn right you shouldn't have." He pointed to his own chest. "You should have said it to me! Jesus, Tom, is it true?"

"Of course it's true! You heard what I said to Ryan…"

"Why didn't you tell *me*?" he cried. "I've just spent the last four days thinking I meant nothing to you. That what you told Ryan was a fucking lie. That everything you said to me was a fucking lie," he said. "And then I have to hear *that* from a complete stranger?" He leaned forward in his chair. "You couldn't even look at me when I walked out of here the other day. You just sat there like I meant nothing to you."

"I didn't tell you because... well, because I didn't know what it would mean to you..."

"It *would have* meant everything to me."

Would have. Past tense. I ran my hands through my hair. I stood up and walked to stand in front of the wall of glass. I turned to face him so he could see the truth on my face. "I'm sorry. I was scared because I'm forty-four and you're twenty-two. You have everything in front of you and I didn't want you to feel trapped." I stopped, and my voice was quieter. "I know what it's like to be young and in a relationship you feel you can't get out of. I've been there, when I was your age, Cooper. I know exactly what that's like, and I want more for you. I don't want you to get to forty and have regrets."

"Tom, I might be young. But I know what I want," he told me. "I want a career. I've worked fucking hard for it."

My heart sank, and I nodded.

"I also want you."

My heart leaped in my chest.

Then he said, "But you need to stop going on about our ages. The age difference has never been an issue for me, you know that." Then he added, "And, Tom, there are going to be differences between us. We like different things— different music, different food, different clubs. We have different friends; we have different ideas on a lot of things. There's going to be things that clash, but that doesn't mean it's wrong."

"I know," I agreed quietly. "I like the differences between us. You've opened my eyes to a lot of things I thought I missed."

"I like the differences too." He smiled and leaned back in the chair. "We're like a retrofit project, making the older, classic style integrate with the modern. When everything says we probably shouldn't gel, we just seem to work."

I looked at him. He *understood* me. Like no one else ever had. It was the perfect analogy. "We *are* a retrofit project. *You* are the perfect retrofit for me."

He stared at me for a long moment, then slowly walked around my desk and stood in front of me. He cupped my face in his hands. "You're the perfect retrofit for me too."

My eyes closed, and I sighed into the palm of his hand. Then his lips were soft against mine, and I threw my arms around him so I could kiss him back. So I could bury my face in his neck and hold him, and he seemed to hold me just as tight. He felt so good against me. No, not good. Right. He felt so *right* against me.

But then he pulled back and put his hand up. "Just so you know, I'm still kind of pissed off at you, but I'm sure I can think of some ways you can make it up to me."

"Anything."

His face was expressionless, but his eyes were serious. "Don't ever make decisions that affect me without asking me first. Ever. That's a deal-breaker, right there. You need to talk to *me*, Tom, about things like feelings and shit. Not someone else."

"Okay," I conceded. "But to be fair, you never talked to me about how you felt either."

He raised an eyebrow at me. "I didn't go talk to your prospective employer and tell her that you have feelings for me," he countered. "And these 'feelings'"—he quoted the air

—"that you keep talking about, you still haven't said what they are."

"I really like you, Cooper," I told him honestly. "Maybe it's more than that, I don't know. But I know I *want* more than that with you. I want everything with you."

He smiled. "Thank you, Tom. Maybe I want more than that with you too."

I couldn't stop smiling. "Really?"

"Don't get too smug, Mr. Elkin. I'm not done with the conditions." He took a deep breath. "I won't move in with you. It's far too soon for that," he said, and my heart sank. "But I'm open to the whole boyfriend thing."

I grinned at him. "Really?"

"Yes, really," he said, and I leaned in to kiss him, but he put his hand to my chest to stop me. "You said you didn't want to hide anymore. Well, neither do I. If we are going to do this, we do it openly. Like we were in Sydney. I want *that* with you. And, now that I'm not working here," he said with narrowed eyes, "we have no reason to hide."

I was grinning hugely. "I agree."

His lips twisted as he tried not to smile. "There's one more condition, Tom. And it's the most important."

I was almost too scared to ask. "Yes?"

He looked at me and a slow smile crept across his face.

WE WALKED out of my office, and Jennifer took one look at us and smiled. "I'll be finishing up for the day," I told her. "If anything is urgent, delegate it to one of my team. They'll handle it just fine."

Jennifer gave a polite nod. "Of course. Can I do

anything for you?" she asked. "Order a lunch? Reservations anywhere?"

"No, thank you, I think we'll be okay."

"I'm glad to hear that," she said. Then she looked at Cooper. "Mr. Jones, it's a pleasure to see you again."

"As always, Jennifer," he replied with a knowing smile.

We walked to the elevator, not holding hands, but when the elevator doors opened, I put my hand on the small of his back as he walked in. He stood a little closer to me than would be considered friendly, and he took a deep breath and smiled.

"What was that between you and Jennifer?" I asked.

One corner of Cooper's lips curled into a smile. "When I got here this morning, I asked if I could see you without an appointment."

"And?"

"She's always been so snarly with me..."

"Did she say no at first?"

"Not exactly," he answered. "She told me it depended on what I was there to say. She said if I was there to make you happy, I could see you right away, and if I was there to upset you any further, I could sit in the hall and damn well wait."

I chuckled. "Wait for how long?"

"I didn't ask," he answered. We stepped out of the elevator and walked through the busy lobby. "But I got the feeling it would have been a while."

We walked out onto the sidewalk, into a rush of people. A warm thrill coursed through me when Cooper took my hand, and as we weaved our way through the crowd, he said, "Anyway, I told her good news was subjective to what the recipient wanted to hear."

I laughed at him. "She would have loved that."

"I thought she was going to call security," he admitted cheerfully. "But she didn't even glare at me. She smiled sweetly and told me that the recipient, meaning you," Cooper explained with a squeeze to my hand, "was miserable without me."

"Is that what she said?" I asked.

"Yep. Miserable, she said. Were you, Tom?" he asked, looking at me.

I stopped in the middle of the sidewalk, not caring about how the people had to go around us, and looked at him. "I was pathetic. It was disgraceful."

Cooper smiled beautifully. "So, maybe you do like me more than just a little."

I slid my thumb along his jaw and nodded. "Maybe I do."

Cooper leaned up on his toes and pecked my lips. "Good." Then he looked over his shoulder, to the front door of my apartment. "You ready?"

I rolled my eyes. "It's not me I'm worried about."

I LED THE WAY, walking into the lobby of my apartment, holding Cooper's hand. We were both smiling, though Cooper's grin was somewhat larger than mine. Lionel stood by the reception desk, watching us curiously as we walked over to him instead of the elevators.

"Lionel." I greeted him seriously. "I'd like to officially inform you that Mr. Cooper Jones has free access to my apartment. He can come and go as he pleases and doesn't need you to buzz him through."

Lionel barely nodded. "Very well."

"Is that it?" Cooper asked rather disbelievingly. "That's all there is to it?"

I looked at him, trying not to smile. "Yes. It's done."

"Well, that's not as satisfying as I thought it would be."

I chuckled, and with a sigh, I looked to Lionel. "You have spare keys to my front door?"

"Yes, sir," Lionel answered. "We keep keys in case of an emergency."

"Would you be so kind as to give one to Cooper?"

Lionel disappeared behind the marble reception desk, and Cooper looked at me. He never said a word, but he rocked up on his toes and grinned. Lionel reappeared and held out a gold key for Cooper.

Before taking it, Cooper looked at him. "This isn't a key to the janitor's closet, is it?"

Lionel smiled. "No, sir. It's not."

Cooper took the key, then looked at me and smiled. I thanked Lionel, took Cooper's hand, and led him toward the elevator. "We better see if it works," I told him. He was trying not to smile in the elevator, and once he opened my front door with his very own key, I asked him, "Is that better?"

"Much better," he said, grinning, as he slid his arm around me and kissed me soundly.

"Does that mean you'll leave my poor doorman alone now?"

Cooper grinned. "Absolutely not."

I couldn't help but sigh. "You'll turn me gray."

"Gray*er*," he corrected. "Now come on, we're going to walk down the street as a couple. You can hold my hand in public, then you can buy me lunch."

I pecked his lips. "You're a bossy little shit."

Cooper kissed me with smiling lips. "I know. It's a Gen Y thing. You'll get used to it."

He pulled the door shut, pocketed the key, and we headed back down to the lobby. As we walked out, Cooper grinned at Lionel, who gave me a smile and a nod, and when we walked out onto the New York sidewalk, Cooper held his hand out. I took it immediately, and he smiled his smug little smile.

He walked up the street like he owned it. He was so confident, so quietly sure of who he was, what he wanted, and where his life was going. He was sexy as hell, had a smile that stole my breath, and mischief in his eyes, and for some unfathomable reason, he wanted to be with me.

I'll get used to it, he'd said.

Would I? Could I?

Cooper squeezed my hand to get my attention. "You okay, Tom?" he asked with a smile. "Because if you're having second thoughts, I'd hate to have to give Lionel back that key." Then he stopped walking and stared at me. "Hey, has anyone else ever been given a key?"

I tried not to smile. "No, only you."

Cooper huffed indignantly. "Just as well. I'd hate to think Lionel gives them out to just anyone."

I laughed at him. "God forbid. I'd hate to think the world revolved around anyone else but you."

Cooper smiled happily. "See? You're catching on with the Gen Y thing already."

He pulled on my hand and led me across the street to some restaurant that had caught his eye. He walked us up to the reception desk and smiled at the maître d'. "Table for two, please."

"Certainly," the man said. "What name?"

Before I could answer 'Elkin,' Cooper said, "Jones."

Would I ever get used to him? The attitude, the snarkiness, the sass, the damn Gen Y thing that drove me insane? I doubted I'd ever get used to it, but it was going to be a lot of fun finding out.

~The End

OUTTAKE

Cooper

The thing about relationships was that there had to be compromise. And I had to remind myself of that as Tom and I walked into the art gallery. There was some art exhibition opening that Tom insisted he take me to, so I was putting on my grown-up face and doing the grown-up thing.

Well, that wasn't entirely true. I might have griped about it, and I might have possibly pouted. But I went.

I also wore the gray suit pants that hugged my ass and the fitted charcoal-colored vest that I knew Tom fucking loved. He never said he did, but he almost swallowed his tongue every time he saw me in it.

I figured if the art exhibit sucked, at least one of us would have something good to look at.

But Tom was excited about it, and that was hard to downplay. It was a joint exhibition opening on expressionism and abstraction, and that, in itself, surprised me. I would have assumed he'd be more into the classics, but no, of course not. I probably shouldn't have been surprised. He was a paradox, that was for damn sure.

He said I kept him on his toes, when really, the opposite was true.

Thomas Elkin was by far the most intriguing, most intelligent, most confident man I'd ever met. Most guys my age mistook confidence for arrogance, but there was something sexy as hell about a guy whose confidence commanded presence. And Tom had it. He was all suave and distinguished without even knowing it. People stared at him—of which he was oblivious—but they knew class when they saw it.

And he was mine.

The great Thomas Fucking Elkin looked at me like I lit up his entire world.

And I'd have been lying if I said that didn't trip my ego. I mean, how lucky was I?

When we walked into the gallery—which kinda looked more like a nightclub than my assumed pretentious art gallery—most of the women and some of the men looked him up and down, undressing him with their eyes. Yet the only one he saw was me.

"People are staring at you," I whispered.

Tom looked around, and of course all the people pretended not to be staring at him.

He looked down at his suit jacket for a stain or whatever. "Why?"

He really was clueless. "Because you're you."

He shook his head, dismissing me. "Don't be absurd."

We stopped at the first painting. "Speaking of absurd..."

Tom chuckled. "Behave."

We stood in front of a wall with a painting that looked

like it had been done by a five-year-old. Monkey. A five-year-old monkey who had been given a box of Crayola, a blank canvas, and LSD. "I thought it was illegal to give primates illicit drugs."

Tom cocked his head at the painting, then slowly turned to look at me. "What?"

Now it was my turn to laugh. "Never mind."

But Tom was transfixed by the painting. He stared at it for a long time, tilting his head a little but never taking his eyes from the messterpiece in front of us. I stood diligently beside him, letting him view it in silence.

I'd never been an art lover. Graphic design, yes. Put me in a museum or a gallery of architecture, and I'd love every minute. But the love of paintings and sculptures had always eluded me. Sure, I could appreciate art for what it was, but I was by no means an art connoisseur.

Tom, on the other hand, was taken with it. We moved on to the next painting, then the next, and he stood quietly, just taking them in. Two were bright colors, one with free-formed strokes, the other with layered squares that formed a bigger picture. The third was a black, gray, and white piece, with nothing but vertical stripes that somehow made the shape of a man's head. A striking red splatter made it look like the man had blown his brains out.

Nice.

Tom gave it equal admiration as he had the druggo-monkey-painted piece and the I-fell-into-a-tub-of-LEGO-bricks piece. He breathed in deep like he inhaled the meaning of life. "What do you make of it?" he said, giving a gentle nod to the painting.

"It's... nice," I allowed, "in a *Silence of the Lambs* kind of way."

Tom snorted but still didn't take his eyes off the painting. "I will never stop being surprised by what comes out of your mouth."

"Well, it's explicit," I amended. "And confronting."

"Isn't that the beauty of art?" he asked.

I considered this. "True. I mean, there's no real purpose to art, apart from aesthetic value."

Tom turned quickly to stare at me. The look on his face was one of shock. "No purpose?"

"No, don't misunderstand me," I tried to explain. "I can appreciate art as much as the next guy, but art, regardless of medium, is just to be looked at, yes?"

Tom frowned a little and turned back to the painting. "The purpose of art is to make us question and feel. To evoke emotion and memories, hopes and sorrow."

I looked at the painting of the man with his brains smeared across the canvas. "And what does this one say to you? And you can't say last week's episode of *CSI*."

He chuckled again. "Why do you assume it's violent?"

"The man has red splatter exploding from his skull. Red is the color of blood," I countered, "and the head wound suggests blunt force trauma."

"Red is also the color for passion and love. Maybe it's his thought process," Tom allowed. "Maybe it's emotion, passion and exuberance, too wild to contain. Maybe the artist's muse comes in pulses."

I looked at the painting. Nope, still didn't see it.

Tom put his arm around my shoulder and leaned into me. "Is it not the beauty of interpretation? What you see is so different to what I see, and *that* is the beauty of art."

I looked at the paintings we'd already seen. It wasn't easy to explain what I didn't like about it. I shrugged. "There's no structure. There's no confines and no direct objectives."

That made Tom grin. "And that's what I love about it." He laughed at my expression. "Think about what we do as architects. Everything is bound by design principles. If not building regulations, then the city's legislation molds what we can and can't do. Hell, even the laws of gravity curb our creativity. Sure, we can pretty up the façade, add some angles, and change some basics, but the fundamentals will always be the same."

"Function, practicality, and affordability," I added.

"Exactly," Tom said. "Even what you're doing at Arlington, which is a huge leap from what I do at Brackett and Golding, will still have to comply with fundamental building codes." He looked at the paintings and smiled. "But these... these are a creative free-for-all. There are no boundaries. The artist is free to create whatever they want."

Hmm. I could see his point, and maybe, just maybe, I might agree with him. "I still prefer my creations to have a purpose, a functionality. And preferably one that's sustainable and leaves the smallest carbon footprint it can."

Tom threw his head back and laughed. "Ah, you really are a true architect."

"I'm also awesome, dashingly handsome, and incredibly good in bed."

He snorted. "You forgot modest."

"Well, I can't be everything. I am but one man."

"Yes, yes you are."

"I am a well-hung man, but one man nonetheless."

Tom smiled a happiness that seemed to come from within. "I'm sure the universe couldn't cope with two of you. Lord knows I couldn't."

With a laugh, I grabbed his hand and led him into the next room. "Come on, show me what you think of the next lot."

There were more paintings in the next room. Each was vastly different, bold colors, no colors, free-formed, straight-lined, oil, watercolor. Tom admired each one, explaining to me what he saw in each piece. I had to admit, I was starting to appreciate art. Or maybe I was just enamored with how he described it, how his mind interpreted different things.

In the next room were free-standing sculptures. While he admired the artwork, I was stuck staring at the gallery-provided seat. Or maybe it was an art piece. I wasn't sure.

It was black leather, a low ottoman at one end, which rolled like a wave to waist height. It was smooth and somehow resembled black water. And all I could think about—

"Do you like it?" Tom asked beside me.

"Yes," I said, still looking at the furniture piece. "I was just imagining all the positions you could put me into on this thing. I could be on my knees at this end while you stand behind me, or you could bend me over the taller end. God, you could just pin me to it and try to fuck me into it."

Tom cleared his throat, making me look at him. Or, rather, at the now-blushing waiter who was holding a tray of champagne flutes.

"Hi," I said, taking a glass. "I was just discussing the functionality of this piece."

He chuckled a little, blushed some more, and went on his way. I shrugged at Tom. "He was totally picturing us fucking on the chair."

Now Tom blushed a little. "Maybe he was picturing you with him, not me." Like it was inconceivable anyone would find him attractive. Jesus, this man was fucking blind.

"I dunno. Have you even seen yourself lately? In case you haven't noticed, you're really fucking hot," I told him, making him duck his head. "And for the record, I don't share my things. And that includes you. You can ask my brother, Max. No one touches my things."

"Is this you putting down an exclusivity clause?"

"Hell the fuck yes. I didn't realize I had to. When I said I'd do the boyfriend thing, I assumed it was all-inclusive, terms and conditions apply, that kind of thing."

He was staring at me, the kind of dark and stormy stare that normally ended with fucking. The kind of eyes that made my skin flush warm and made my dick twitch. "I don't want anyone but you."

"Good."

"Thomas Elkin?" someone asked.

Tom and I both turned to the sound. It was a woman, possibly fifty years old, and from her clothes and jewelry, and even her makeup and hairstyle, I could tell she was wealthy. "Alexandra Armitage," Tom said. "What an unexpected pleasure!"

"Oh, Tom, you're looking fabulous," she said, kissing both his cheeks. "Tell me, who is this handsome young man?"

"This"—Tom put his arm around my waist—"is Cooper Jones, my boyfriend."

"Oh," she said, her perfectly manicured eyebrows raised. Whether she had any clue Tom was even gay or she was just shocked because of our age difference, I didn't know. I also didn't care.

Then Tom explained, "I worked with Alexandra and her husband to get their apartment on East Seventy-First remodeled."

God, how the rich socialites of New York City loved having their prestigious addresses mentioned in conversation. She beamed. "And what a marvelous job you did."

"Thank you," Tom said graciously.

She looked at the black leather chair we were standing in front of. "Interesting piece. Like a modern take on a Victorian chaise."

"A retrofit, of sorts," I mused. "A contemporary twist on a classic. I like the sound of that."

Alexandra said her goodbyes, and Tom hid his smile behind his champagne glass. "A retrofit, huh?"

"It always comes back to us, don't you think?" I finished my glass of Moët. "What I really want to get back to is the way you were looking at me before we were so rudely interrupted."

"The way I was looking at you?"

"Yes, all smoldering eyes, like you wanted to see just how many positions this sofa actually has."

His gaze intensified, but it wasn't quite smoldering. "Is that so?"

"Yep. I mean, we could try the sofa at home." I stepped right in close and whispered, "I'm pretty sure you could bend me over that and fuck me until I pass out."

And there it was. Smoldering eyes and flared nostrils and the softest, sexiest, bitten-back groan that seemed to pulse in my cock.

He snatched up my hand and stuffed me into a cab, not even caring that the cabbie got a peep show of us making out in the back seat. Fuck, this was so hot.

Thankfully Lionel had gone home for the night, and the other doorman didn't care that Tom and I didn't exchange pleasantries. As soon as the elevator doors were closed, Tom pushed me against the mirrored wall and ground our hips together as he kissed me. My head was spinning so much with lust and pleasure, I almost couldn't stand upright. And when we arrived at our floor, he dragged me inside, only to leave me standing just at the front door. He stalked off toward our room, and come back out a few seconds later with a bottle of lube and a foil packet. And a seriously fucking determined look on his face.

"The couch," he demanded.

I complied, walking around to the back of the sofa, moaning as I pressed my cock against the hard leather. I slowly leaned forward so my ass stuck out and rubbed myself against the sofa. The friction felt so good.

The anticipation of what was coming felt even better.

Tom stood behind me. "Like this?"

"Yes."

He put the lube and condom on the back of the couch, where he could grab them easily. But then he put his hands to my front and roughly pulled me back against him, deftly undoing my button and fly. He slid my trousers and briefs down over my ass, pushed me forward against the back of the sofa, and ran his hands down my back to my ass. The cool lube drizzled down my crack, then skilled fingers rubbed all around my hole before inching inside me.

But it wasn't what I wanted. I wanted his thick, hot cock inside me. "Tom, please." I snatched up the condom and ripped it from the wrapper. I knew how lube-slicked hands made it impossible to unwrap them, so I did it for him. The sound of his zipper made me moan.

"Want it that bad, huh?"

"Mmm," I answered, rubbing my cock against the back of the sofa. "Fucking hurry up, Tom."

He pressed his left hand between my shoulder blades and pushed me down and forward. His right hand gripped my hip and I held onto the seat with both hands. My pants were still around my thighs, and Tom's were only just undone. There was no time for undressing, or perfect, or considerate. I wanted him to fuck me, and fuck me hard, and so God help me, he was going to. The blunt head of his cock nudged against my ass and he pushed inside.

"Oh fuck," I cried out.

He slid all the way, using both hands on my hips to grip me. He took a moment for me to get used to the intrusion before he started to move. He was slow at first, then he thrust a little harder, making my toes leave the floor, but his fingers bit into my hips, pulling me back onto him. I groaned with every thrust, and he grunted as he gave it to me.

This was fucking.

This was pure need and no niceties required.

This was hot.

Then his grunts got louder. "This is what you wanted," he huffed. Every thrust felt like it was deeper, harder.

"Yes," I cried. There was something about being fucked like this. Turning him on so much he couldn't even get undressed, he needed to bury his cock inside me so bad his pants were still around his hips. "Fuck yes."

He groaned long and loud. "I'm gonna come in you." He gasped, and with one long, deep push into me, he stilled. I could feel him swell inside me as he came, pulsing in time with his grunts and cries. Eventually he slowed and fell forward, still inside me. He wrapped his arms around my chest, his breath hot on my back.

"Fuck," he mumbled. "You okay?"

"Mmm," I hummed. "I am, but you need to power up, old man. Your work here isn't done. I'm so fucking hard and you're gonna take me to bed and finish me off, okay?"

He smiled against my back and huffed out a laugh. "You'll be the death of me."

"No, I won't," I told him. "But you have to admit, it'd be a helluva way to go."

~Fin

ABOUT THE AUTHOR

N.R. Walker is an Australian author, who loves her genre of gay romance. She loves writing and spends far too much time doing it but wouldn't have it any other way.

She is many things: a mother, a wife, a sister, a writer. She has pretty, pretty boys who live in her head, who don't let her sleep at night unless she gives them life with words.

She likes it when they do dirty, dirty things... but likes it even more when they fall in love.

She used to think having people in her head talking to her was weird, until one day she happened across other writers who told her it was normal.

She's been writing ever since...

Contact the author:
nrwalker@nrwalker.net

The Spencer Cohen Series, Book Two

The Spencer Cohen Series, Book Three

The Spencer Cohen Series, Yanni's Story

Blood & Milk

The Weight Of It All

Perfect Catch

Switched

Imago

Imagines

Red Dirt Heart Imago

Free Reads:

Sixty Five Hours

Learning to Feel

His Grandfather's Watch (And The Story of Billy and Hale)

The Twelfth of Never (Blind Faith 3.5)

Twelve Days of Christmas (Sixty Five Hours Christmas)

Translated Titles:

Fiducia Cieca (Italian translation of Blind Faith)

Attraverso Questi Occhi (Italian translation of Through These Eyes)

Preso alla Sprovvista (Italian translation of Blindside)

Il giorno del Mai (Italian translation of Blind Faith 3.5)

Cuore di Terra Rossa (Italian translation of Red Dirt Heart)

Cuore di Terra Rossa 2 (Italian translation of Red Dirt Heart 2)

Confiance Aveugle (French translation of Blind Faith)

A travers ces yeux: Confiance Aveugle 2 (French translation of Through These Eyes)

Aveugle: Confiance Aveugle 3 (French translation of Blindside)

À Jamais (French translation of Blind Faith 3.5)

Cronin's Key (French translation)

Cronin's Key II (French translation)

Au Coeur de Sutton Station (French translation of Red Dirt Heart)

Partir ou rester (French translation of Red Dirt Heart 2)

Rote Erde (German translation of Red Dirt Heart)

Rote Erde 2 (German translation of Red Dirt Heart 2)